Mates, Dates and Diamond Destiny

Cathy Hopkins lives in North London with her handsome husband and three cats. She spends most of her time locked in a shed at the bottom of the garden pretending to write books, but is actually in there listening to music, hippie dancing and talking to her friends on e-mail.

Occasionally, she is joined by Molly, the cat who thinks she is a copy-editor and likes to walk all over the keyboard rewriting and deleting any words she doesn't like.

The other cats have other jobs.

Barny likes to lie on his back in the grass, stare at the clouds and create poetry. (Sadly, none of it has been published, as it has been hard to find someone to translate it from Catspeak, but he and Cathy are ever hopeful.)

Maisie, the third cat, was worried that Cathy may have forgotten what it is like to be a teenager, so she does her best to remind her. She does it very well. She ignores everybody and only comes in to eat, sleep and occasionally wearily say 'miwhhf' (this means 'whatever' in Catspeak).

Apart from that, Cathy has joined the gym and spends more time than is good for her making up excuses as to why she hasn't got time to go.

Mates, Dates and Diamond Destiny

Cathy Hopkins

PICCADILLY PRESS • LONDON

Thanks to Brenda Gardner, Yasemin Uçar, Jon Appleton,
Melissa Patey and the rest of the team of fabsters at Piccadilly.
To Rosemary Bromley at Juvenilia. To Steve Lovering for his
constant support and help on all aspects of the book and
for being such a good pal.

First published in Great Britain in 2005
by Piccadilly Press Ltd.,
5 Castle Road, London NW1 8PR
www.piccadillypress.co.uk

A catalogue record for this book is available from the British Library

ISBN: 185340 876 X (trade paperback)

1 3 5 7 9 10 8 6 4 2

Printed and bound in Great Britain by Bookmarque Ltd
Typeset by Textype Typesetters
Cover design by Jo Grey

Set in 11.5 Bembo and Tempus

Papers used by Piccadilly Press are produced from forests grown and
managed as a renewable resource, and which conform to the
requirements of recognised forestry accreditation schemes.

Chapter 1

Smug Slug

'I bet you can't do it,' said Tony.

'How much?' I asked.

'A pound every time you mention one,' he said.

'Done,' I said. 'Prepare to hand over all your pocket money.'

'Pfff,' smirked Tony. 'It's going to be like taking candy from a baby.'

I was sitting with my brother Tony in the Costa coffee bar in Highgate waiting for my mates on Saturday morning. We'd got into an argument and he'd bet me that I couldn't last a day without talking about boys. Thankfully Izzie, Lucy and TJ arrived soon after so I didn't push his face into his plate of panini and tomato, something I was very tempted to do.

'Are you two fighting again?' asked Izzie as she slid in next to me while Lucy and TJ sat on either side of Tony. 'We could feel the vibes from back here when we were getting our drinks at the counter.'

'He said that I had nothing going on in my head apart from boys, boys and boys,' I said. 'Blooming cheek.'

Izzie, Lucy and TJ exchanged looks as if to say that they agreed with Tony.

'Hey come on, guys,' I said. 'Give me a break. I know I'm not Einstein but . . .'

'But Tony's right, Nesta,' said Izzie. 'You are our current boy expert of North London, England . . .'

'The world, the universe, etc.,' TJ finished.

'Yeah,' said Lucy, '*and* you did put boys down as one of your hobbies on that questionnaire we had to do for Miss Watkins in PSHE.'

Tony was grinning like a smug slug. I don't know why some people find him attractive when he is clearly an annoying pain in the butt. I suppose he is the standard tall, dark and handsome but beauty's only skin deep and on the inside lurks his true self, which is a repulsive reptile. Sadly I am the only person who can see this, which is one of the many reasons that I am so misunderstood.

'OK,' I said, as I stirred the last remnants of my hot chocolate, 'so yes, maybe boys do occupy a small part of my mind but I'm a fifteen-year-old girl, get real. I just can't believe his cheek in insinuating that's *all* that's going on.'

'You're right,' said Tony. 'Sometimes you think of handbags or pointy shoes.'

I lifted my hand to punch him but Izzie caught my wrist.

'He doesn't mean it, Nesta,' she said. 'He's winding you up. Now kiss and make up. You two children have got to learn to play nicely.'

'No way,' said Tony as I stuck my tongue out at him.

'I wouldn't worry,' said Lucy. 'My brothers say far worse things to me.'

'Well, you would say that,' I said. 'You always stick up for Tony.'

'I do not.'

'Do.'

Tony put his arm round Lucy and gave her a squeeze and she smiled up at him. Sadly she can't see his true nature, no matter how many times I've warned her. She only sees love god. It's very sad, although no one's too sure what's going on with them lately. Are they an item or not? Some weeks they are, some weeks they're 'just good friends'. At the moment, they're 'just good friends'. Good friends who snog a lot, if you ask me.

'I do *not*,' Lucy insisted. 'I stick up for whoever I feel needs sticking up for at the time.'

I pushed out my bottom lip in the hope that she could see that I needed sticking up for. I felt betrayed by her lack of support. And Izzie and TJ hadn't exactly come forward to my defence either. Grrr, but I'm feeling cross with everyone today, I thought, as I ate the last piece of my chocolate pastry. Must be my hormones. My period started this morning and that always makes me feel cranky and prone to axe-murdering anyone who comes within five yards. I've tried taking painkillers for it but for me, chocolate seems to be the only thing that offers any relief.

So far, I'd had Coco Pops, two hot chocolates and the pastry but I still felt out of sorts. And no doubt all the sugar would result in me getting an almighty great spot on my forehead or chin. Sometimes it sucks being a girl.

'OK then, Lucy,' I said, 'it's the Easter hols in a couple of weeks. What if in the holidays, Tony and I were taken ill with the same kidney disease and the only thing that could save us was you donating one of yours, which one of us would you give it to?'

Lucy started laughing. 'But you're not dying of kidney disease. And neither is Tony.'

'Hypothetically.'

'Stupid question,' said Lucy.

'OK, your last Rolo then. Who would you give your last Rolo to?'

'Um. I'd give you half each.'

Typical Lucy. She'll never take sides with anyone if she can help it.

'So what did you mean when you said that your brothers used to say worse things to you, Luce?' asked TJ.

Lucy blushed. 'They used to call me Nancy No-tits.'

I sighed heavily. I knew what they were trying to do. They were trying to change the subject, divert Tony and me from annoying each other. Huh. My mates: Lucy the joker, always trying to smooth things over with a laugh. TJ the diplomat, always trying to ensure that we're all communicating. And Izzie the mystic, feeling our vibes before we've felt them ourselves. I wouldn't know a vibe if it was served up deep fried with chips and peas. Izzie's always thinking deep thoughts about the universe, life, God and stuff. That's not me at all. Waste of time, I think. Who knows why we are here or what for? We might as well just get on with it and have as nice a time as we can. That's my philosophy. Sometimes I wonder where I fit in with the three of them, especially when they start having their 'deep' conversations.

Not that I can't talk or don't have anything to say for myself. In fact I often talk too much. I'm a stick-my-foot-in-it with my big mouth type person. At least everyone knows where they stand with me, though. What you see is what you get. Simple and uncomplicated. I don't think that makes me an airhead. Those are the other things Tony calls me: Big-mouth and Airhead. Not very flattering. Oh God. Maybe they all hang out with me out of pity. Their good deed for the week. Or maybe, my mum and dad have paid them to be my friends. God it's sad when actually I'm quite a nice person deep inside. At least *I* think I am.

'What's going on in your head, Nesta?' asked Izzie. 'You look miles away.'

'Um . . .' I wasn't sure myself. Sometimes I think some really insane thoughts I wouldn't want to share with anyone. Normally I can be really cool and in control but these days, when I've got my period, I turn into someone who is likely to cry at the drop of a hat or kill someone for saying something annoying, and God only knows what madness might come out of my mouth if I'm not careful. I put on my best 'deep thinker' look so that hopefully Izzie wouldn't spot that I'd turned into psycho girl.

'Oh you know, just thinking . . . about life and stuff,' I replied. 'So what other names did your brothers call you, Luce?'

Lucy blushed. 'Squirt. Short-arse. At least Tony has never called you a name like that.'

Tony was looking so smarmy and pleased with himself that I decided to blow his cover. 'No? So what about Airhead? Maggot brain? Nappy bucket? Slimeball? Droopy drawers . . .? The list goes on and *on*.'

'That was when you were little,' said Tony. 'All I said this time was you think about boys a lot. All the time in fact . . .'

'As usual, no one realises that actually I think really deep thoughts,' I objected, 'and there is a hell of a lot that goes on in my head besides boys.'

'So prove it,' said Tony. 'As I said before your mates arrived, I bet you can't do it.'

'Do what? Bet her what?' asked Lucy.

'My dingbat of a brother has bet me that I can't go a day without mentioning boys. And I have accepted the challenge. You guys can be my witnesses.'

'Yeah, but it's not just a general wager,' said Tony. 'It's specific. She has to give me a pound each time she mentions a boy, boys in plural or in fact any reference to boys at all.'

'Just Nesta?' asked Lucy. 'The rest of us can talk about boys?'

Tony narrowed his eyes and peered at Lucy in what I can only suppose he thought was an attractive manner. I thought it made him look like he was about to fall asleep. 'OK. These are the rules. Izzie and TJ can mention boys as much as they like. Nesta can't or if she does, she has to pay up. For you Lucy, it's different. For you, there is only one boy on the planet. And that is me.'

Lucy punched him playfully, laughed and gazed into his eyes. Really. Those two are vomitous when they're together. It's enough to bring up your breakfast.

'So what's on the agenda?' asked Tony. 'What are you girls going to do today? Isn't Saturday the day for you all to be TV stars?'

He was referring to the TV pilot that Izzie, Lucy and I were in last weekend. It was for a show called *Teen Talk*, a discussion programme about issues that affect teenagers.

'That was just the pilot. The series isn't due to start until September or October,' said Izzie.

'And was there any talent there?' asked Tony with a sly look.

There had been lots of boys there and I was about to jump in and give him the details when I saw TJ shaking her head at me.

'Didn't notice,' I said. 'And don't think that you can trick me into talking about the forbidden subject, *mon frère stupide*. We may be related but quite clearly one of us is far superior in the brain department.'

After that it was war. Tony did everything he could to get me to mention boys or refer to them in some way but I can be a good match for him if I want and I wasn't going to give in easily. After a while, the lady behind the counter at the front of the café started giving us a 'you've outstayed the allotted time to drink one drink in here so if you're going to stay, buy something else' look. It was time to go or else we'd end up frittering all our pocket money away on hot chocolates.

'OK. So, top five interests?' asked Tony as the lady behind from the counter came over to clear our table. 'Izzie?'

'Astrology, music, aromatherapy, witchcraft and boys,' said Izzie. 'And chocolate.'

'That's six,' said Tony, 'but I'll let you have it. TJ?'

'Er . . . reading, boys, music, movies, sport.'

'Lucy?' asked Tony.

Lucy gave him a coy look. 'Boys, definitely . . . er, fashion, movies, travel . . . although I haven't done a lot yet, it is going to be one of my major interests and . . . cooking.'

'Cooking!' said Izzie. 'Since when have you been into cooking?'

'Since those two gorgeous Italian guys got their own TV show,' she replied. 'Oh yes, cooking is well up there on the list.'

'I can cook,' said Tony. 'And I'm Italian. I told you that you didn't need to look anywhere else. So . . . what about you, Nesta?'

All eyes turned to me. I knew that by leaving me to last that he was trying to lull me into a false sense of security and that I'd blab out . . . boys. But I wasn't going to fall into his stupid little trap.

'Quantum physics, history, particularly the period between 1824 and 1828 in . . . er . . . Russia. So that's two. Um. The science of amoeba reproduction. Egyptian hieroglyphics, period between 4 and 5 BC and finally . . . b – b – bo – botulism, the study of infected sausages.'

Lucy, Izzie and TJ cracked up and even Tony almost laughed. As we were messing around, I noticed a boy with ginger hair and glasses come into the café with a collection tin. It looked like he was asking the manager for permission to take it round, and a moment later, he started going from table to table asking for money. We were sitting at my favourite table at the back so we were out of his way. We always sit there because it gives us the best view of who's coming in the door and as Costa is a café much frequented by the boys from Highgate School, it's a good vantage point for surveying the talent.

I nudged Izzie to look at the boy. Most of the customers waved him away. 'That charity collector isn't having much luck is he?' I said being careful not to say the word 'boy'.

'I feel sorry for him,' said Izzie. 'It takes a lot of nerve to go round people you don't know asking for money.'

'I feel sorry for the customers in here,' I said. 'All they want is to have a cup of something on a Saturday morning in peace and someone's bothering them to give away their money.'

'Don't be so tight, Nesta,' said Izzie in what I thought was an unnecessarily cross manner. 'They only have to give some loose change, and it's probably for a good cause.'

'Probably for a good cause,' I mimicked. 'I bet his mum has made him do it anyway . . .' I was about to continue and object that I wasn't being tight, when Lucy elbowed me in the ribs.

'Ohmigod. Eyes right,' she said. 'Door. Look who's just come in.'

I turned to see who she was talking about and my stomach tightened. It was William, a boy I'd met just before Christmas last year. He was a friend of Luke de Biasi's (otherwise known as love rat extraordinaire). For a while I had considered getting serious with Luke (i.e. going out longer than three weeks). But then he got into TJ as well (behind my back) and she thought he was The One. She fell for him really badly. It was an awkward time for all of us and got really complicated with no one knowing who had said what to who. It almost split us up as mates as Lucy took sides with me and Izzie took sides with TJ. In the end, we all realised that it wasn't worth losing our friendship over a boy who told lies. I met William after it was all over with Luke. A cutenik by anyone's standards. I remember wishing that I'd met him before Luke. But I didn't. Bad timing. And he's still Luke's mate as far as I know. So strictly out of bounds as far as I'm concerned. Shame.

I quickly turned away so that he didn't catch me staring but not before I'd noticed that he seemed to be looking for someone. I sat up straight, flicked my hair back and put my chin down so that if he saw us, he'd get my best angle. When I looked over at him a few moments later, he seemed not to have noticed us at all as he was heading for the boy with the collection tin. And then I saw that William had a similar tin and after exchanging a few words with the ginger-haired boy, was heading for the back area of the café. As he did the rounds of the tables, all the girls on the various tables perked up and within seconds, he had them reaching for their purses. He did look good, in fact I remember TJ saying that he could be Orlando Bloom's younger brother. I'd say a cross between Johnny Depp and Orlando. Same great cheekbones and he'd grown his hair since I'd last seen him and now it was on his shoulders, giving him that Victorian poet look that I'm into these days.

'I can't believe the effect that boy is having on the females in here,' I said. 'It's pathetic.'

'Pound,' said Tony.

'What for? Why?'

'You said "boy". You can't believe the effect that boy . . .'

'Oh for heaven's sake, Tony. Get a grip. I wasn't exactly talking about *boy* boys, I was merely commenting on the effect that William was having on the girls in here.'

'Another pound.'

'Why? I didn't say boy then.'

'You said William,' said Tony. 'That's a boy's name.'

'Now that's being *stupid*,' I said. 'I've got to be able to say people's names. I don't know what's the matter with you today.'

Tony looked shocked. '*Me*? *You've* been in a weird mood all morning. You've argued with every single thing I've said.' Suddenly he slapped his forehead. 'Oh . . . I know. Should have guessed. Have you got your period?'

A wave of fury went through me and this time I really was ready to sock him. I *hate* boys who assume that just because you're a bit off with them that it's because it's that time of the month. Even if it's true.

At that moment, William appeared at our table, smiled a hundred watt smile and held out his tin.

'Collecting for the . . .' And then he *finally* noticed me. He narrowed his eyes in a manner not unlike the way that Tony had for Lucy only five minutes ago, only when William did it, it made me want to slide to the floor, wrap myself around his ankles and say, 'Take me, I'm yours.' He said, 'We've met before, haven't we?'

I was about to be all cool and say that I didn't remember when Izzie piped up.

'End of autumn term show last year,' she said. 'The mayor's project about London.'

William turned to TJ. 'Yeah course, you were on the history team with my sister Olivia and my mate Luke.'

'Umf, niwih,' said TJ. Poor TJ. She was looking at the floor as though she wished it would swallow her up. She never said much about the Luke affair once it was over but I got the feeling that it affected her more than she let on. Izzie told me that she genuinely thought that Luke was her soul mate and that up until she'd met him, she thought soul mates were a load of rubbish. She needed rescuing from William's spotlight gaze.

'Yes, how is Luke?' I said tossing my hair back and almost hitting Izzie in the eye. (That's another thing that happens when I have a period. I get clumsy and my co-ordination goes to pieces.)

'Good. Great. Shall I tell him you asked after him?'

'As *if*,' I said with as much disdain as I could muster. I hadn't meant to ask after Luke. It had slipped out before I could help it, when I saw TJ looking uncomfortable.

'What's your name again?' asked William.

Unbelievable, I thought. He hasn't even remembered my name and to think that I spent two nights having major snogging fantasies featuring him when I was falling asleep.

'Eleanor,' I said.

William looked puzzled. And so did Tony, Izzie, Lucy and TJ.

'Eleanor? Hmm. Strange I didn't remember that as Eleanor's

my sister's name as well. OK. So *Eleanor* . . . I'll tell Luke that I saw you, but that you made it clear that you weren't asking after him.' His tone of voice suggested that he was laughing at me in some way.

'Your sister's not called Eleanor,' I said.

'Er . . . *my* sister. *I* ought to know.'

'Ah, but you just said you remembered TJ from the project she did with your sister *Olivia*. You can't catch me out.'

William looked at me as if I was really dim. 'Duh. I wasn't trying to catch you out. Why would I want to do that? It is possible to have two sisters, you know. Sometimes people even have three! Olivia's my younger sister. Eleanor, my older.'

I felt a complete idiot. Of course it was possible that he had more than one sister. 'OK,' I said. 'No need to be sarcastic, William . . . oh . . . or whatever your name is . . . I don't really remember . . .'

'It *is* William,' he said as he smiled his hundred watt smile again. 'How *nice* that you remembered.'

Oh God. Now I look *so* uncool. I'd let him know that I'd remembered his name when he'd forgotten mine. And I'd asked after ratfink Luke! Why? Why? Why? Now it sounds like I'm still interested in him. I'm acting like I'm brain-dead. And I think I may be going to blush which is something I *don't* do! Oh why did I say my name was Eleanor? What is *wrong* with me?

And then the worst possible thing that could ever happen, happened. Mary O'Connor, one of our classmates, walked past on her way to the Ladies.

'Hi guys,' she said, coming over to our table. Then she turned to me. 'Hey, Nesta, remind me on Monday. You left your passionfruit and mango body lotion in the showers after gym yesterday. I put it in my locker for you.'

'Oh um, thanks, Mary.' I glanced up at William who looked highly amused; in fact, he looked like he was going to burst out laughing.

'Nesta. *Nesta!* That's it. Now I remember. So, have you changed your name or something or is Eleanor like a nickname?'

'Eleanor?' asked Mary. 'Who's Eleanor?'

Now I knew I was definitely blushing. No doubt about it.

'I . . . I . . .' Stupid, stupid me. *Why* had I lied about my name? It always backfires on me when I lie. Stupid, stupid.

Lucy and Izzie both spoke up at the same time.

'Nesta is her second name,' said Lucy.

'Eleanor is her stage name,' said Izzie.

'Right,' said William. 'Second name. Stage name. So what should I call you?'

I'd had enough of feeling like a prize idiot. I got up and stood directly in front of him. Nice eyes, I couldn't help but notice. Brown with thick black lashes. But still with a look of high amusement that was *very* annoying.

'*You* can call me . . . sir,' I said and turned back to the others. 'And now I'm going to the Ladies.'

'Shouldn't that be the Gents, if you're a sir?' said William with a smirk as he began to move on.

'Thank God he's cleared off,' I said turning back to my mates as he went to the next table. 'Some boys are just so full of themselves . . .'

'Pound,' said Tony.

I didn't care any more. 'Boys, boys, boys. A trillion times. I've said it. So there. What are you going to do? Sue me?'

Izzie chuckled and looked after William who turned and gave me a quick glance up and down. 'Me thinks a leetle spark of fancying going on there,' she said.

'Yeah,' said TJ. 'Eeelectricity. You like him, don't you?'

'No way. I do *not*,' I said. 'I did when we met last year but not now. I can tell exactly what type he is. He's the kind that thinks he's God's gift.'

Lucy nodded. 'She definitely likes him.'

'Eeewww!' I said. 'As *if*.'

What's the difference between a girl with
PMS and a rottweiler?
Lip-gloss.

Chapter 2

PMS

'I'm so short,' groaned Lucy as she gazed at her reflection in the mirror in the Ladies at the back of Costa. 'I hate standing next to you guys in the mirror as then I see how tiny I really am.'

'Small but perfectly formed, oh little one,' said Izzie. 'Unlike me. I'm so freaking enorm—' She was about to go on but Lucy reached up and clamped her hand over her mouth. We'd all told Izzie in no uncertain terms that if she went on about being fat that we would have to kill her. Izzie isn't fat. She's got a great figure. Curvy. But like so many people, she wants to be a stick insect.

'And I'm so ugly,' said TJ as she wet the front of her hair from one of the taps and tried to flatten it down. 'My hair is crazy today. I look as pale as a potato and I've got a spot on the end of the nose. No boy is going to look at me ever again.'

They're bonkers, because all of them are very pretty in different ways. Lucy is blonde with blue eyes and although she is small, like Kylie, she's in proportion. She's been looking great lately and is letting her hair grow after having it short and spiky for ages. Now it's down to her shoulders again and looks really good. Izzie's hair is also to her shoulders but is chestnut and cut in layers. When the light catches it, it has the most amazing glossy conker shine. She also has beautiful eyes. Green and dreamy. She says she got them from her Irish ancestors. (I say in that case, she ought to give them back to them as they might be missing them.) And TJ is a total babe even though she seems oblivious to the fact. Her best feature is her mouth, wide and full plus she has lovely brown eyes and fabulous long, dark hair halfway down her back, which she often wears in a plait (unless we're out pulling boys when she leaves it loose).

I gazed at myself in contrast to them. Coffee-coloured skin because my mum is Jamaican and my dad Italian, long black hair, brown eyes. My mates tell me that I'm the best-looking girl in the school, which is very sweet of them, and I guess I can make myself look halfway decent when I try as long as I don't open my mouth. Last October, I had to have a brace put in and although I try my best to be positive about it, I can't wait until it comes out and I can smile properly at people again without looking like Hannibal Lecter with that wired contraption over his jaw in *Silence of the Lambs*.

I applied my lip-gloss. 'I am gorgeous. I am gorgeous. I am gorgeous,' I said to my reflection.

The others burst out laughing.

'And *sooooo* modest,' said Izzie.

'No. Nothing to do with being modest. How many times do I have to tell you? It's to do with confidence. It's the first thing they teach at model school. Learn to love yourself. Walk tall . . .'

'Yeah right,' Lucy interrupted. 'If only. Not easy to do at five foot one and it doesn't help having mates who are all at least five foot seven.'

'And growing in all directions,' said Izzie before anyone could pounce on her. 'I don't know what I'm going to do in the summer hols. Mum wants a beach holiday but I know what will happen when I get in the sea and the whales see me. They'll all start singing "We Are Family".'

Lucy and TJ cracked up laughing.

'Good one,' said Lucy. 'Must add that to my joke collection.'

'If you think you look crapola,' I said, 'everyone will pick up on it. You of all people should know that, Izzie. You're always going on about positive thinking and I honestly thought you were getting better lately and not being so down on yourself.'

'I am,' said Izzie. 'Sort of. I'm learning to accept myself . . .'

'That's not enough,' I said. 'Come on! After me – all together, a one, a two, a one, two, three. I am gorgeous.'

We all lined up, looked at ourselves in the mirror and chanted. 'I am gorgeous. I am gorgeous. I am gorgeous.'

Izzie and TJ started pulling monster faces at themselves as they chanted and unfortunately one of the customers from the café came in and saw us. She scurried into the nearest cubicle, looking as if she thought that we were mad. She might not be wrong.

'Positive thinking,' I said as she disappeared behind the door and we all burst out laughing.

★ ★ ★

I love Saturdays. It's my favourite day. And I love spending it with my mates having a good laugh and not thinking about anything remotely serious like homework or school and even though I've got stomach cramps today, I'm not going to let that get in the way one bit. It's a funny thing with periods. I remember that before mine came, I really wanted it to happen. Thought it would make me a grown up. Hah! The novelty soon wore off when I experienced what came with it. PMS, headaches, mood swings, cramps. One month, Lucy, Izzie, TJ and I all got our periods at the same time. We laughed about it after but at the time, everyone was majorly oversensitive and tetchy and we almost fell out.

Once we'd done our hair and retouched our make-up, we said goodbye to Tony, who was going off to meet some of his mates and then we were ready to set off down to Camden Lock. It's one of our favourite hang-outs as the shops there are really cool and there are stalls selling everything from bangles and beads to magic mushrooms. One of Lal's mates apparently bought some mushrooms down there last week and was as sick as a dog after taking too many. He ended up having his stomach pumped in Casualty.

TJ went into the newsagent's to buy some chewing gum while the rest of us waited at the bus stop.

'I bet he's only doing it to meet girls,' I said as I buttoned up my jacket to keep out the chilly wind that had blown up whilst we were inside the café.

'Who? What?' asked Lucy.

'That William boy . . .'

'I knew you liked him,' said Lucy.

'Pound,' said Izzie.

'A pound? Whose side are you on?' I asked.

'You said boy,' said Izzie.

'You're supposed to be my mate, not Tony's, so forget about that stupid bet, will you?'

'But we promised to be witnesses,' said Izzie.

I wrapped my arm around her neck and pulled back slightly. 'And I promise that I will kill you if you don't forget it. Understand, *amigo*?'

'Understand,' spluttered Izzie. 'So what were you saying?'

'William. I reckon he only does that collecting money for charity to pull girls.'

'No,' said Izzie. 'I disagree. He's too good looking. He wouldn't need to pull a stunt like that to get a girl.'

'Looks don't necessarily ensure you pull,' I said. 'You have to meet people too and it helps if you have a ready-made opener. He's on to a winner there, I reckon. Yes. Very clever indeed. I should put it on my list of pulling techniques after get yourself a dog.'

'A dog?' asked Lucy.

'Yeah. Look at all the attention we get when we take Ben and Jerry out. Or Mojo.'

Lucy laughed. 'We get attention all right when they've put their noses somewhere they shouldn't be.'

'Dogs are a ready-made introduction,' I said, 'whether they're well-behaved or not. It's the same with collecting for charity. It gives you an excuse to approach cute boys that you might otherwise be shy of.'

'But you're not shy,' said Lucy.

'I am sometimes,' I said.

Lucy looked at Izzie as if to say she didn't believe it one bit.

TJ came out of the shop. 'What have I missed?'

'Nesta saying that she thought William did his charity work as a way of meeting girls,' said Izzie.

'No way,' said TJ. 'No one could be that calculating, could they?'

Izzie and Lucy looked accusingly at me.

'What?' I said. '*What?*'

'*You're* that calculating,' said Izzie. 'You're thinking of doing it as a way of meeting boys.'

'And what's wrong with that, Miss High and Mighty?' I asked. 'You can do good *and* meet people at the same time. And what's wrong with being calculating about meeting boys? Sometimes you have to have a plan. Life is what you make it. And if you do charity, people automatically think you're a good person, so that's a bonus as well.'

TJ looked shocked and shook her head. 'I'm not sure about that,' she said. 'It sounds cold. Like you're using people to make yourself look better.'

'No way,' I objected. 'No way am I a user.'

'Yeah. But don't you think your intentions are supposed to be more sincere?' asked Lucy.

I had a feeling that they were ganging up on me again. I was being cast in a bad light and all because I tried to think up good ways to meet boys. It was so unfair – actually, they should be grateful that I'm so creative in my boy-meeting technique!

'I *am* sincere,' I said. 'I just like meeting boys and this seems like a good way. Two birds with one stone sort of thing.'

'That's true,' said Izzie. 'I guess whatever the reasons someone does charity work, it's better to do something than nothing. In fact, I've been thinking about doing something myself lately . . .'

'Like what?' asked Lucy.

'Dunno. Still thinking about it.'

'We're only fifteen,' I said. 'What can we do?'

'Don't know. But I want to do something. I was watching this programme recently about a country in Africa where they don't have enough to eat; it was really heartbreaking. There were children dying of malnutrition. It made me feel really bad because I'd been so obsessed with food, you know with all the mad diets I was trying. I'd even binned some of Mum's suppers. Suddenly it felt wrong as here on the same planet are people who have nothing.'

'Is that why you wrote that song about people going hungry?' asked Lucy.

Izzie nodded. Izzie wants to be a singer–songwriter when she is older. She plays guitar and writes her own lyrics and sometimes sings with a local band called King Noz. She wrote this great song a few weeks ago about the state of the world and she even got to sing it on the *Teen Talk* pilot when one of the guest singers got stuck on a train and didn't show up.

'I know what you mean,' said TJ. 'It doesn't seem right, does it? I mean, all the resources are there, it's just out of balance. Some countries have too much and some too little.'

'Yeah,' said Lucy. 'Why can't we share out a little more?'

We sat on the wall by the bus stop and talked about some of the problems in the world. Then we were silent for a few minutes while we thought about what a mess the world is in many ways. When I glanced at everyone's faces, they were really gloomy, like it was the end of life as we know it. I hadn't seen Lucy look so miserable since her favourite band, the VIPs, broke up.

'Oh come on, guys,' I said. 'It's Saturday! Time off. Lighten up. Let's talk about something else.'

'Why?' asked Izzie. 'Sometimes I want to talk about stuff like this. It bothers me. I think about it a lot and I think part of the reason that there is such a problem in the world is that people keep ignoring it or pretend it's not happening.'

'But it's making you depressed,' I said. 'Look at your faces. We didn't make everything go wrong so there's no point in going over and over it and getting frustrated. Oh, the state of the world, people are dying, starving . . . oh oh oh . . .'

'Well, they are,' said Lucy. 'I think Izzie's right. I don't think we should ignore it.'

'Yeah,' said TJ. 'I saw a programme last week that really made me sad as well. It was about an orphanage. The children were amazingly brave as most of them had nothing and no one.'

Cue gloomy faces again. Oh God, I want to shoot myself, I thought. The atmosphere was starting to get *really* heavy so I decided to try and lighten it.

'I've got a solution,' I said.

Three faces looked at me eagerly.

'Don't watch the miserable programmes. Watch comedies instead.'

'*Nesta!*' said Lucy. 'Sometimes I think you have *no* feelings.'

'It's not that.' I sighed. 'It's not that I don't care. It's . . . Oh, for heaven's sake, can we just change the subject? I'm starting to feel so miserable. Starving people. Lonely children. There are *other* things happening on the planet, you know.'

Izzie and Lucy were looking at me as if people starving in the world was *my* fault just because I didn't want to talk about it. And TJ was looking at all of us as if trying to work out what she could do to make it all better. What *is* going on today? I asked myself. What had started off as a fun day was turning into grey broody day with everyone touchy and in a weird mood. Even the weather was starting to look ominous with the sky turning greyer and threatening rain. I decided to try again to make them laugh.

'We're all dooooooooomed,' I said in a spooky voice, then mock-strangled myself. I thought it was quite funny but no one else seemed to.

'I don't think we should joke about these things,' said TJ. 'It is serious.'

'OK then,' I said. 'I'll go and do some charity work. I shall try and save the world. Will *that* make you happy and shut you up?'

'You have to want to do it,' said Lucy. 'No point in doing it to prove a point.'

'Yeah. And you just said you only want to do it to meet boys,' said Izzie. 'Maybe Tony was right. Maybe that *is* all that is going on in your head.'

That hurt, and inwardly I winced. What on earth had happened in the last ten minutes? It was like suddenly I was the bad guy and I hadn't even *done* anything. I was simply trying to get them to lighten up. I find it difficult when people start going on about the problems in the world.

What good does it do talking about it over and over? Mum and Dad do it a lot but that's partly because they both work in the media and have to keep up with world events. Mum is a news presenter on cable and Dad makes films and documentaries. They watch a lot of news discussion programmes, and I can see that the subject matter often makes them miserable too.

Usually these programmes show a couple of politicians and a couple of journalists, giving their high and mighty opinions. One jibber jabbers on from one angle, then the other jabber jibbers from the other. Jibber jabber. Jabber jibber. Then they start trying to blame each other for whatever has happened, then a load of people all with different solutions to fix the problem get going, and then *they* all argue and get heated and upset and nothing gets solved. But somehow they all go away feeling better about it because they've *talked* about it. Programmes like that give me an almighty headache. And in the meantime, there are still people starving, dying, homeless or being bombed when they only want to go about their daily lives as normal. By now, I was starting to get depressed myself.

I'd had enough. If Lucy, Izzie and TJ wanted to hang about all day talking about the sorry state of the planet they could, but I wasn't going to do it with them. Plus my stomach cramps weren't getting any better. The idea of going home to my duvet, a bar of chocolate and a hot water bottle was beginning to appeal.

When the bus finally came up the High Street and drew up

at the stop, I waited until Lucy, Izzie and TJ had got on, then stepped back.

'See you later,' I said from the pavement. 'I'm going home.'

The bus driver shut the doors and started off down the road with Lucy, Izzie and TJ staring out of the window at me, concerned and surprised.

As I made my way down the hill to our flat, the skies finally broke and it began to rain. As I hurried along, my mobile rang. I knew it would be the girls but I didn't want to talk to them. Not yet. So I let it go on to voice mail. I felt my eyes well up with tears as I went over what they'd said to me. It wasn't fair. I'm not a bad person. I do care about the state of the world. I *do*. I care that there are lonely people at Christmas and sick people with no one to visit them in hospital and old people with no heating and wars that take away people's homes and disasters that kill loved ones and dolphins that get caught in tuna nets and puppies that no one wants . . .

It was like a dam burst inside me and everything that's wrong in the world seemed to hit me with full force.

I had to sit down in a bus shelter for a while and have a good cry while I waited for the storm to blow over. Luckily there was no one around so I was able to let rip.

Got no feelings, huh, Lucy Lovering?

Don't care, huh, Izzie Foster?

Can't ever be serious, huh, TJ Watts?

Well *look* at me now, I thought as salty tears dripped down my cheeks and onto my chin. What a shame they can't see me this upset. Yeah. If they saw me now they'd see just what a serious, sincere, caring, feeling person I really am.

Out of the corner of my eye, I saw a group of cute looking boys coming down the hill so I quickly pulled myself together. It was one thing wanting my mates to see what a caring sharing person I really am, but boys can get put off by any display of intense emotion, especially when they don't know you that well.

Plus crying makes your eyes puffy. Not a good look in my book.

What does PMS really stand for?

Psychotic Mood Swings

Pardon My Sobbing

Pass My Sweatpants

Permanent Munching Spree

Puffy Mid Section

Pass Me the Shotgun

Pimples May Surface

People Make me Sick

Charity
muggers

'Nesta, the girls are here,' Mum called from the front door later that afternoon.

A moment later, Izzie, Lucy and TJ trooped in to our living room where I was curled up under my duvet on the sofa watching *Breakfast at Tiffany's*, starring Audrey Hepburn.

'We're soooo sorry about earlier,' said TJ, flopping herself down at the other end of the sofa.

Lucy knelt on the floor and put her hands together as if in prayer. 'Yeah,' she said. 'Sorry, sorry, sorry. We were mean, nasty friends and we were horrid and you didn't deserve it. All you were trying to do was get us to lighten up.'

Izzie held up a carrier bag. 'We bring peace offerings,' she said and started pulling things out of it. 'The home PMS kit. Every girl should have one. Numero one. V. important. Chocolate.' She handed me a Snickers bar.

'Number two, the ultimate feel-good movie,' said TJ, reaching into the bag and producing a DVD. '*It's a Wonderful Life*. We know it's one of your favourites so we dropped back to Lucy's to pick it up from her mum's collection of oldies but goldies – and I know it's supposed to be a Christmas film and it's almost Easter, but who cares?'

'Yeah,' said Izzie and she began singing. '*We wish you a Merry Easter, we wish you a Merry Easter, we wish you a Merry Easter and a Happy New spring, summer, autumn, winter and . . . New Yeeeeeear.*'

I shook my head. 'Mad,' I said. 'Beyond help.'

Lucy put her hand in the bag. 'And I brought you this as well,' she said as she produced what looked like a little bag covered in flowery material. 'It's a wheat bag. Dad's just bought a load of them for his shop. Supposed to be brilliant. It's got all sorts of healing herbs in it and you put it in the microwave for a few minutes. It heats up like a hot water bottle and smells fab. I'll go and do it.'

And off she went to the kitchen.

'And we also got you some aromatherapy oils,' said Izzie. 'Ginger. Camomile. Ylang ylang. All good for period pains. I'll go and make a compress in the bathroom. Back in a mo.'

And off *she* disappeared.

'Wow,' I said. 'What's come over you lot?'

TJ started gently massaging my feet under the duvet. 'It was when we got on the bus and saw you standing there on the pavement. You looked so sad and we got talking about it in Camden, and Izzie said that it's all very well being concerned about people suffering in far away countries but you have to be aware of people on our doorstep. She thought that we'd upset you and you were probably having a bad period so we decided to come over and make it better.'

'So what you're saying is that *I'm* a charity case?'

TJ grinned. 'Exactly. And a head case. But we won't go into that at the moment.'

I grinned back at her. I was so glad they'd come to see me and didn't hate me after all.

A few minutes later, I was settled back on the sofa watching the movie. I had the wheat bag on my back, a warm scented compress on my tummy, TJ massaging my feet while Lucy and Izzie sat on the floor and handed me pieces of Snickers bar. Heaven. Happy, happy, happy.

Over the following week, even though my sanity returned, I felt like the whole world was conspiring against me. Everywhere I went I was accosted by people collecting for this charity, for that charity, for the homeless, the sick, the blind, the handicapped, the deaf, the abused, the hungry, the rainforest, for the dolphins, old donkeys, almost-extinct monkeys, dog homes, cat homes . . . The charity muggers were everywhere: hovering on the High Street, outside the supermarket, inside the supermarket, in pub doorways, on the pavement outside school. Waiting to pounce. It's not that I hadn't noticed them before. Of course I had and sometimes I gave some spare change, sometimes I didn't. Sometimes I just wanted to go down to the High Street and not be bothered by them. And that's just how it was when I gave money, if I'm honest. A way of not being bothered. I gave them money to leave me alone. Mostly I didn't even notice what they were collecting for or who they represented – at least not until now.

'Maybe the universe is trying to tell you something,' said Izzie on Tuesday evening after a man collecting for the homeless had accosted me outside Marks and Spencer in Muswell Hill.

'Like what?' I asked.

'Only you can know that,' she said in her Mystic Iz voice, which is deep and mysterious . . . and very annoying as often I don't have a clue what she's on about.

There was no let-up at home either. Just when I thought it was safe to think about something different, appeals came flying through the letterbox reminding me once again that out there people needed help. Letters asking for sponsorship for a child here, a child there. Charity Christmas cards on sale even though it was only March. Single mothers with no money, children without parents, old people without company, children without schools, villages without water . . . The list seemed endless, and I was starting to get seriously depressed about it. Images of the homeless and hungry were beginning to haunt me at night.

Even the telly was no escape. I was just settling down to the soaps on Wednesday night when the ads came on and it started all over again. People in need were sandwiched in between the commercials encouraging viewers to buy, buy, buy or eat, eat, eat. What a mad, mad, mad world, I thought.

'Mum,' I said when she came in to sit down and join me in

watching telly, 'do you think I'm an ignorant person?'

'Oh yes,' said Mum with a solemn expression. She curled up in the armchair next to the fireplace. She put her glass of wine on the bookshelf next to it. '*Really* ignorant.' I knew she didn't mean it because she couldn't keep a straight face and burst out laughing. 'Why do you ask?

'Been thinking. I mean, do you think I'm selfish and only think about myself?'

Mum took a sip of her wine. 'You're a *teenager*,' she said. 'Comes with the territory. All teenagers are self obsessed know-it-all horrors . . .'

'Wow. Don't hold back, Mum,' I said. 'Say what you really mean!'

'Only kidding. No, Nesta. I don't think you're selfish or ignorant. I think you're lovely. Why are you asking?'

'Just . . . well, lately it's like I've noticed – you know – all the people in the world who need help. And up until this week I haven't even given them a second thought, which is why I thought that maybe I'm ignorant. Selfish. I mean, how could I have not noticed before? I've been living in a bubble, blind to the needs of people around me . . .'

'I wouldn't go that far, love . . .'

'Izzie said that maybe the universe is trying to tell me something. That I've begun to notice for a reason.'

'A reason? Like fate or destiny?'

'Yeah. Maybe it's my fate.'

'OoooKaaaaay,' said Mum. 'And what do you think your fate might be?'

'Not entirely sure yet, but I think it's that I need to do something. Find a cause. I haven't got one. Have you got one?'

'Yes. I sponsor a child in India and I give to vari–'

'See! *See!* You give. You have a cause and I didn't even know. Seems everyone has been doing good all around me and I've been the only one in the middle of it all doing nothing but thinking of myself. Oh *God*. I must be the worst person on the planet. That's why I think I'm so ignorant!'

'You're not ignorant. You're only fifteen . . .'

'I need a cause. My own thing.'

'OK. No problem. Any ideas?'

'No. Not sure yet but one thing is for certain and that is that I can *never* be the same again. No. My eyes have been opened. I have to change. Make amends. I *have* to do what I can to change the world.'

Mum took a large gulp of her wine and looked anxious.

'Right,' she said.

At that moment, Dad came in to join us.

'What are you two talking about?' he said as he sat on the sofa with me.

'Nesta's going to change the world,' said Mum.

'Oh,' said Dad, then he chuckled. 'God help us.'

DIY feel better kit for period pains and mood swings

Chocolate

Feel-good DVDs (*It's a Wonderful Life* is our current fave)

Wheat bag or hot water bottle

Comfy jim-jams

Aromatherapy oils for a compress or a bath:
ylang ylang, ginger, camomile.
To make a compress is really simple, just put some
hot water in a bowl, add 4-6 drops of the oils and
swish them around. Soak a flannel in the scented water then
apply to the achey part.

For an aromatherapy bath: add 4-6 drops of the essential oil
to the bath water when it's running, then swish it around
so that the oils don't remain in one part (they can sting in
such a concentrated form).

Mates to make you laugh when feeling glum.

Good
works

'What on earth is going on?' asked Tony the following evening as he stepped over the pile of bin bags that I'd put in the hallway.

'Stuff for the charity shop,' I said. 'I've been doing a clear out. You should do the same since you have loads of stuff you don't need.'

It was only a start but the idea had come to me in maths that afternoon. I'd been racking my brains to try and come up with some way that I could start my good works and it came to me as Mr Hall was droning on about some boring maths equation. I could give away all the stuff I don't use to charity. That was it. Obvious!

I raced home to get started and once I'd begun, it seemed that just about everything I had wasn't really needed. Mum would be delighted as I have the reputation as the hoarder of the family. Usually I can't bear to let anything go. But not today.

I'd pulled out everything from the top of my wardrobe, from my chests of drawers, under my bed. There was all sorts of rubbish stored away in boxes and bags: all my Barbies, My Little Pony dolls, my princess doll, teddy bears, fluffy rabbits, cassettes, videos, DVDs, CDs, books, bits of jewellery, clothes I'd only worn once. Shameful, I told myself as I hurled it all into bags. It's about time I did this.

Tony had a peek in one of the bags. 'But there are loads of good CDs in here. Surely you're not giving these away?'

'Oh yes I am. I don't need them. I have too many things.'

'Are you on *drugs*?' asked Tony as he continued to sift through the CDs I was chucking out. 'You never give anything away and these are all your favourite CDs. And – I bought you this one last Christmas and . . . here's the one Lucy got you. Hey, you can't get rid of these. They were presents.'

'I don't need them. I don't need most of the things I have. From now on, I'm going to live a much simpler life.'

Tony looked at me as if I had lost my mind. 'Excuse me, but you are Nesta Williams, aren't you?' he asked. 'Or have you been possessed by an alien who's eaten your brain?'

Mum came in the front door and, like Tony had done, almost tripped over the bags.

'What's all this?' she asked as she took her jacket off and put her keys on the hall table.

'Nesta's giving away all her worldly goods and going to be a nun,' said Tony. 'But can I keep the CDs? She won't need them in the nunnery and she has a few I haven't got.'

'No way,' I said. 'They're not for you. They're for the needy.'

'Don't be mad. The charity shops will sell them for ten pence each. Tell you what. I'll give you a fiver for all of them and you can give that to the charity of your choice.'

'What? Er . . . OK, as long as I can still listen to them when I want.'

Tony rolled his eyes and Mum started having a root through the bags. She didn't look very happy with what she found in there. She picked out a jumper that she bought me a few months ago. 'Why are you getting rid of this? It's almost new.' She continued sifting and saw that I had put the contents of most of my wardrobe in. 'Nesta, take this stuff back to your room this instant. This is ridiculous. You're giving all your clothes away. What are you going to wear?'

'Sackcloth and ashes,' said Tony. 'Our Nesta's seen the light and has become a freaking saint.'

'Go on, laugh. I might have expected that from you,' I said. 'When have you ever done anything for anyone else?'

'Now enough of that, Nesta,' said Mum. 'Haven't you ever heard the expression "charity begins at home" and you having a go at your brother isn't very charitable.'

Tony stuck his tongue out at me from behind Mum's back so I made a rude hand sign back at him.

'And that certainly isn't very nice,' said Mum.

'But he started it. . .'

'Oh for heaven's sake, both of you, grow up.'

'I was only trying to do something good,' I said, 'and it's taken me ages to get all this bagged up.'

'Too bad,' said Mum. 'There are some almost new things in

these bags and you're not giving them away until we've been through it all together so that I can see what you want to get rid of. Now, tidy up this mess before your dad gets home and take all these bags back to your room.'

Tony made a smug face at me and luckily this time Mum saw him.

'And you can help her, Tony.'

'But . . .' he started.

'NOW!' said Mum.

At supper that night, I tried out my next good idea to help the poor by suggesting to my family that we cut down on our grocery bills and donate money spent on unnecessary items and treats to charity. It didn't go down too well.

'Get lost, Nesta. If you want to go without then you can, but don't bring in the rest of us,' said Tony.

'Yeah, but I read that five pounds could feed a child for a whole month in some countries.'

Tony rolled his eyes and helped himself to some ice cream.

'Like that ice cream,' I said. 'Do you really need it?'

'*Muuuum*,' groaned Tony. 'Tell her to get off my case will you?'

'Nesta,' Mum started. 'Don't you think you're being a little excessive?'

'A *little* excessive?' said Tony. 'Understatement!'

'Go on then stuff your face. Go on. Ignore all the millions of starving people . . .'

Tony got up from the table and went to the door taking the

ice cream with him. 'I'm not sitting here listening to this . . .'

'Why? The truth makes you uncomfortable does it?'

'Nesta, lose the Mother Teresa routine or go and live somewhere else,' said Tony. 'Get real. First, you go on at me about not giving all my stuff away and now I can't eat in peace. Trying to make me feel bad, telling me what everything cost and what could be done with the money. What do you want me to do? Starve? Then will you be happy?'

'No. Not starve, but maybe we don't need to consume as much as we do. We're a society of consumers. That's why there's the imbalance . . .'

Tony sighed heavily. 'What is with you? Up until last week you were Queen of the Consumers and proud of it. In fact if I remember rightly, your motto was "when the going gets tough, the tough go shopping". You weren't exactly thinking of the poor and hungry when you bought those silver snakeskin heels or that little top from Morgan were you? And now, just because some boy you fancy collects for charity, you think you have to do the same, no doubt so that you can impress him next time you see him.'

'That is soooo not true. And I don't fancy him!'

'Who?'

'William Lewis.'

'Ah,' smirked Tony, 'but you knew exactly who I was talking about, didn't you?'

Mum and Dad didn't say anything. They just looked at each other and Mum raised an eyebrow.

Sometimes I hate Tony. Now Mum and Dad think I'm only

worried about the state of the world because of some boy. Like I don't have a mind of my own.

'Are you going to finish that?' asked Mum, looking at the bowl of ice cream she'd put out for me.

I dipped my spoon in. Butter pecan. It did taste good. And it wasn't exactly as though I could put a tub of ice cream in an envelope and post it to a poor country. Maybe I'll have to think of another way of donating money, I thought as I finished the bowl. It didn't seem that it was going to come out of the housekeeping.

After school the next day, I took the one bag of stuff that Mum was allowing me to give away up to Muswell Hill. It was a lovely evening and after all the rain and chilly winds we'd had recently, at last I could feel spring in the air. I stood by the zebra crossing and wondered which charity shop to give it to: the one for cats, for cancer, for old people or for the hungry in Africa? Oh God. It's impossible to make a decision like that. I put my bag on the pavement and tried to make up my mind which was going to be *my* charity.

Maybe I could persuade Izzie, Lucy and TJ to give some of their old things away too, then we could divide our stuff between them. Yes, that would solve the problem and nobody would get left out. I popped into Sainsbury's and asked if I could have a couple of carrier bags, then sat on the kerb and sorted my things into two bags.

Unfortunately a group of lads passed by as I was dividing my stuff up.

'You look kind of young to be a bag lady,' one of them called over. 'Come with us and we'll give you a good meal and somewhere warm to sleep!'

'Yes. We've got a big fat sausage and a bed for you,' called another as his mates sniggered behind him.

Sad, I thought as I ignored them and continued dividing my clothes up. Some boys really don't have a clue. As if I'm going to respond to a chat-up line as stupid as that. We've got a big fat sausage for you? Duh. How pathetic can you get?

When I'd finished sorting, I took one of the bags to the nearest charity shop and gave it to the lady behind the counter.

She gave me a really sweet smile. 'Thanks so much dear,' she said. 'We do appreciate it.'

I left feeling really good and walked out to the Broadway where there were the usual posse of collectors hovering outside the shops by the zebra crossing. I found my purse and instead of trying to avoid eye contact as I usually do, I walked up to them and gave them some spare change. Outside Ryman's, I gave fifty pence to a man who was collecting for the disabled. And by Marks and Spencer, I put the last of my change into a homeless man's cap. By the time I had reached the bank at the roundabout where I was meeting Izzie, TJ and Lucy, I was beginning to feel positively saintly as everyone I gave money to beamed at me as though I was the only person who had donated anything that day.

'Hey guys,' I said to the girls who were already waiting for me.

'Why are you carrying your charity shop stuff?' asked TJ.

'I thought you were up here giving it away.'

'I gave half of it away,' I explained then quickly asked if they would have a clear out too so that all the shops would get something.

'Yeah, that's a good idea,' said Izzie. 'Plus all the books on Feng Shui say that it's really good to clear out any clutter.'

'But you have to decide where to take it,' I said.

'All of them need stuff,' said Lucy.

'Yeah. And that's the problem,' I said. 'I need to decide which is my charity. And seeing as I intend to be a celebrity when I grow up, it's probably a good idea to decide it now . . .'

'Why's that?' asked Lucy. 'What's being a celebrity got to do with it?'

'Obvious,' I said. 'You must have seen celebs when they're on TV raising money. It's never a general thing, like, "Oh just give the money to whoever needs it." Oh no, they all seem to have a particular cause in mind.'

'Like Bob Geldof with Band Aid,' said TJ. 'That was after he saw a programme about the plight of Ethiopia.'

'Yeah, that was brilliant,' said Izzie and put her hand on her heart. 'Sir Bob. Respect.'

'Yeah. See. He knew what his cause was. And maybe that's part of growing up,' I said. 'Part of discovering who you are. Just as you are identified by the car you drive, the clothes you wear, the drink you drink, you ought to have your own personal charity as well.'

'There's an article about Star Axford in my last *Vogue*,' said Lucy.

'God, I love her,' said Izzie. 'She's so beautiful. And so glamorous. And her dad is Zac Axford.'

'Who's he?' I asked.

'Zac Axford? Big rock and roller. He was huge in the Eighties. My dad has all his old albums. The family are mega loaded. They always appear on those England's richest people lists that are sometimes in magazines. Star's mum was a model too. The whole family sounds fab!'

'So what has this got to do with charity?' I asked.

'Apparently Star gives away ten percent of her earnings to charities,' said Lucy.

'Exactly,' I said. 'See, all the cool celebs do it.'

Izzie rolled her eyes. 'But you make it sound like having the right handbag or trainers,' she said. 'Like a designer charity. The latest accessory to make you look good.'

As usual my good intentions are being taken the wrong way, I thought.

'No. I didn't mean it like that,' I objected. 'Just I want to . . . oh never mind. I just think it's brilliant giving to charity. Makes you feel good.'

'So does a muffin and a hot chocolate,' said Lucy. 'Let's go to Costa. I'm starving.'

'Yeah,' chorused Izzie and TJ.

'Oh . . . but I've no money left,' I said as I realised that I'd given all my pocket money away.

Izzie nudged Lucy. 'Looks like we have our own charity case here. Don't worry. We'll pay for you.'

'You don't need to do that,' I said.

'Why? Too proud to accept our donation?' teased Lucy. 'As you said, it's great to give and sometimes being on the receiving end can be hard. Humbling.'

'Yes, but no, but . . .?'

'Yeah,' said TJ. 'We can't have something and let you just sit there and watch. No, come on, we'll club together.'

'No, I meant you don't need to do that, because maybe you should give the money for the hot chocolate to charity like I did,' I said. 'You don't really need it and the few pounds you'd spend in the café, you could give to a good cause.'

TJ, Lucy and Izzie looked at each other and then at me.

'Oh hell.' Lucy sighed. 'I'm confused now. I feel bad. I *do* want a hot chocolate. I was looking forward to it but I also think I ought to give my money away like you did, Nesta and I'll feel like I'm selfish or something if I don't. Oh stinkbombs . . . Why did you have to go and bring all this up? It's made things really complicated.'

'I know what you mean,' said TJ. 'Now I feel like I'm a bad person too. I feel rotten because I don't want to give my pocket money away. I don't get much and to tell the truth, if I gave what I do have away, I'd only be doing it because now I feel guilty and I don't want you to think badly of me.'

'Hhm,' said Izzie. 'Something's weird about this. The vibe isn't right any more and I'm with TJ, Nesta, I feel guilty too. We all do, so we wouldn't be able to enjoy getting a hot chocolate any more. You know what, guys? Suddenly I don't feel like hanging out. I think I'll go home. Think about it. See you all later.' And off she went towards the bus stop.

'Me too,' said TJ. 'I think I'll go and take Mojo for a walk.' And she went to join Izzie.

I turned to look at Lucy who shifted about on her feet and stared at the pavement.

'Me too,' said Lucy. 'Sorry, Nesta. Dunno why, but suddenly I feel *really* depressed.' She dug her hand into her jeans pocket and handed me two pounds. 'Here. That's all I have. Give it to whatever cause you want. Catch you later.'

Off she went, and I could tell by the way she hunched her shoulders as she walked away that she was fed up.

And so I was left standing on my own and the rosy glow I'd experienced earlier had completely disappeared. I give up, I thought. Do nothing and everyone thinks I don't care. Do what I can and everyone gets depressed and hates me. I can't win. I don't know how Sir Bob Geldof did it when he got all those pop stars to give their time and money. He must have been very persuasive or put it differently as I'm sure no one had a go at him for making them feel guilty. I don't know. Maybe I'll go and have a cappuccino. Oops. Can't. No pocket money left and it would be wrong to use Lucy's money. As I watched Izzie and TJ get on the bus that would take them towards Finchley, I felt totally confused. Trying to do good is clearly not as easy as it first appears, I thought as I walked back up the Broadway and gave Lucy's coins to the man collecting for the disabled. He beamed a thank you back at me but this time, it didn't make me feel so good.

£5 a month will help two children at a school
in Ethiopia complete their education.

£10 can pay for three text books for school
children in Zambia.

£20 can feed three children who have lost their
parents to AIDS in Malawi for a month.

£50 can pay a trainee teacher's salary in Kenya for a month.

Bin bag hell

Lucy called a couple of hours after I got home.

'Is that Saint Nesta?' she asked when I picked up the phone. 'Feeder of the hungry, healer of the sick, benefactor of the poor?'

Phew, I thought. She can't be that mad at me if she's making jokes.

'It is,' I said. 'And pray, what dost thou want, oh sinner?'

'I may have the solution.'

'Solution to what?'

'Your sudden need to get involved in charity. I was telling Mum and Dad about what happened in Muswell Hill and Dad had an idea. You know his shop is next door to one of the charity shops?'

'Yeah.'

'Well, he says that they're often looking for volunteers there.

Mrs Owen, the lady that runs it, was looking for people to help tomorrow as she's been let down by a couple of her usuals.'

'Tomorrow? Wow. That would be cool. Working in a shop.'

'No. Not working in the shop. You're not old enough to work out the front. She wants people in the back to sort through the donations for a jumble sale in Kilburn on Sunday. She said that they're desperate for people to go through the bags and see what's there, what's to be chucked and what can go to jumble.'

'I could do that,' I said. 'You do mean tomorrow?'

'Yeah.'

'All day?'

'Yeah. Until four. I was telling Mum and Dad about you wanting to do something and giving away your pocket money and they both said that at our age, we're probably better off giving our time and energy. What shall I tell Dad, so he can let Mrs Owen know?'

'That I'll be there,' I said. 'What time?'

'Nine-thirty.'

'Right.' Nine-thirty on a Saturday. Bummer. I'd have to get up early but I'd do it. Lucy's parents were right. Using my time did seem like a better idea than giving away all my pocket money and losing my friends over it.

'And Nesta . . .'

'Yeah?'

'I'll do it with you, because even though you were an almighty pain before, laying such a guilt trip on us all, I would actually like to do something as well.'

'Top. It will be a laugh.'

'And Izzie wants to come too.'

'Izzie? Is she still mad with me?'

'Nah,' said Lucy. 'She looked up your horoscope. Some planet's square with another one or something. You'll have to ask her but she said the stars explained why you've been a bit over the top lately.'

'Good. Thank you stars. I hate it when you're all cross with me. How's TJ?' I asked. I knew that they'd all have been texting or e-mailing about me behind my back.

'TJ has footie practice in the afternoon and has to work on the school mag with Emma in the morning. But she's cool about you, although she said she did still feel a bit confused and not sure what's she's supposed to do to help the world. Said she's going to think about it, and on the one hand, she feels guilty that she has so much, like a home and a bed and food and clothes, but on the other hand, really glad she does. I guess we all have to find our way round this – although my mum came out with one of her quotes that kind of made sense.'

'What was that?' I asked. Lucy's mum works as a counsellor and collects great quotes and sayings that she can use in her work to make a point or cheer someone up. Some of them are really inspiring.

'I was telling her that in the face of all the trouble in the world I feel helpless. Like I'm too small to do anything and I don't mean my height.'

'Yeah. I know what you mean. It's like, where do you start?'

'Anyway,' Lucy continued. 'Mum said that there's a saying that goes something like, anyone who thinks that they're too small to make a difference should try sharing a bed with a mosquito.'

'Hah right! Cool. Yeah. Let's bzzz, baby.'

Lucy, Izzie and I were at the charity shop on the dot of nine-thirty the next day. A little old lady with white hair who was wearing bright pink lipstick let us in and introduced herself as Mrs Owen. She led us through to the back where there was a small room, stuffed wall to wall and floor to ceiling with black bin bags.

'Some of this has been here for months without anyone looking at it,' she said as she indicated the bags. 'We haven't enough volunteers, so it's just been left. Anyway, see what you can find. Put it into piles of books, games, toys, bric-à-brac and clothes and so on, then box them. Someone's coming to collect some of it later on. Keep the really good or designer clothes for the shop, medium good clothes for the jumble, and the rubbish can be chucked out.'

'Right, will do,' said Izzie.

'And one of you can make some tea for the shop workers,' said Mrs Owen. 'Doris and Lilian will be in shortly.'

'Is it possible to open a window somewhere?' I asked. 'It's very hot in here.' I had put a fleece on when I got dressed as it was chilly then, but already the day was warming up. I hadn't thought to wear anything underneath so that I could strip off later. Of course, Izzie and Lucy both had brains and had thin crop tops on underneath their jackets.

'Sorry, love,' said Mrs Owen. 'It's because of the boiler next door and it's always on for the water. It does tend to heat up in here and there's no window or door to let any air in. Nothing we can do, I'm afraid. See if you can find an old T-shirt you can put on in one of the bags. In fact, you don't want to ruin your nice jeans either so if you find an old pair of trousers or shorts, just slip them on as well.'

'Thanks,' I said. 'I might do that.'

Lucy went out to the small kitchen to be shown tea duties while Izzie and I took a bag each and began sorting. I looked for something I could change into while I worked. It made sense to get out of my normal clothes.

Mrs Owen had been right – the bags had been there for ages and some at the back were covered in dust. 'Poo-eeee,' said Izzie, holding her nose after she'd opened the first bag. 'This one stinks.' She pulled out the clothes in it and they were filthy. Whoever had donated them clearly hadn't washed them before handing them in, and the room began to smell of stale sweat. Ucky. No way was I going to wear any of these clothes, not even for doing the sorting.

Lucy took tea through to the shop and then brought us a mug each. 'The *girls* have arrived,' said Lucy indicating the shop where there were now three white-haired old ladies behind the counter. 'They're discussing Lilian's recent varicose vein operation so I didn't hang around. Oh, and she said we should take lunch at twelve-thirty.'

Izzie pulled her mobile out of her back pocket. 'I'll let TJ know. She said she'd come and meet us on our break.'

I scraped my hair back into a scrunchie so that it didn't get in my way and started to sift through the clothes. First we threw the contents of a few of bags into the middle of the floor and began to look through. Not a clean T-shirt in sight, only old shirts and horrible looking jumpers. Then Lucy opened a new bag and pulled out a piece of fabric and held it up.

'Here,' she said with an evil grin. 'This will do for you to wear.'

It was an old-fashioned-looking orange sundress with purple polka dots and a sailor collar. The sort of dress that normally I wouldn't be seen dead in, but at least it was clean and with no sleeves, it was the lightest thing we'd seen so far. No one was going to see us; it would do fine. So I took my clothes off and wriggled into it while Lucy and Izzie cracked up laughing.

'Well, it's *different*,' said Lucy as I modelled the dress for them and did a twirl. 'Sort of Minnie Mouse style.'

'Oh, who cares,' I said. 'It's like an oven in here. I'd have died if I'd kept my fleece on.'

I did feel better in just the dress and we got stuck into the task at hand with gusto. It was really hard work sorting everything into boxes to be taken away for the jumble sale, and by twelve o'clock my back was beginning to ache. Plus it got hotter and hotter until it was like a sauna in there. I felt like I was dripping sweat. None of us could believe some of the stuff that people had handed in. Paint-stained, mud-marked, worn through, with holes in, reeking of stale cigarette smoke. Only occasionally was there a bag with pristine clean clothes and they of course went straight on to the 'shop' pile.

'I think I'm going to pass out,' said Lucy after one particularly stinky bag. 'This is bin bag hell. Why don't people just chuck this stuff instead of bringing it here and wasting people's time?'

'Yeah, whose mad idea was this?' asked Izzie as she leaned back and stretched her arms above her head. 'Maybe donating your pocket money isn't such a bad idea after all, Nesta. I think I'd rather have given someone a couple of quid if only I could have stayed in bed this morning.'

'I know, I know. Sorry,' I said as I wiped my forehead with the back of my arm. 'God, it's so hot in here. Good job there's no one to see us looking such a sweaty mess.'

I piled what seemed like the hundredth bag of stuff on to the floor and we began to sift through a treasure trove of stuff from the Sixties and Seventies. There were some hideous white plastic hoop earrings, lime green and yellow striped tights, an orange mini skirt, a pink Afro wig and a pair of turquoise and maroon platform boots.

'Be great for a fancy-dress party,' said Lucy.

I shook my head. 'Anyone would look like a complete eejit in that get up,' I said. 'I mean, a party is a party and whatever the theme, you still want to look halfway decent. In that outfit, you'd never pull anyone.'

'It's twelve-thirty,' Mrs Owen called from the shop. 'Take half an hour, girls.'

'Phew,' said Izzie as she headed for the door. 'Let's get out of here!'

Lucy didn't need much prompting either and followed her straight out. I was about to change back into my jeans and fleece but I felt so sweaty that I didn't want to wear anything so warm until I'd cooled down a bit. It would be OK to pop out in the dress for a short time. It looked like the day had turned into lovely sunshine outside.

TJ was waiting for us by the flower bed outside Ryman's. She looked so cool in her jeans and a white tank top.

'Hey, guys,' she said, then burst out laughing when she saw me. 'Hmm, a new look, I see.'

'Yeah. Like it?' I asked as I gave her a twirl. 'Polka dot and orange is the new black.'

'How's it going in there?' she asked.

Lucy pulled a grim face. 'Not great. Like a prison sentence in fact. *Not* a lot of fun.'

'We all got hard labour,' said Izzie, 'but we're hoping to get time off for good behaviour.'

I felt bad since they wouldn't have been there if it hadn't been for me making them feel guilty. And, if I was honest, I wasn't exactly enjoying myself either, even though I kept telling myself that it was all for a worthy cause.

'What have you been up to?' asked Izzie. 'Magazine stuff?'

'Yeah. Actually, I've had a great morning,' TJ replied. 'I had a long hard think about all this charity lark last night. I'd felt confused after . . . well . . . you know . . .'

'After I'd made you all feel guilty,' I said.

TJ smiled. 'I'm sure you didn't mean to. But anyway I decided, I can write. Maybe I can write something that will get people thinking or raise awareness or something. I talked it over with Emma and she agreed. A series of articles on various aspects of charity would be great for the magazine, plus it will give the different causes some exposure.'

'What a brilliant idea,' said Lucy. 'So what are you going to do first?'

'Something to draw the readers in. I reckon if we went in with a heavy article about the state of the world – you know, all gloom and doom and making people feel bad – it might turn people off,' she said. I swear Izzie gave me a meaningful look at this point. I smiled back at her like I didn't know what she was on about (though I knew exactly).

'I suggested we start with a guide to the charity shops in North London,' TJ continued. 'That's where I've just been. Some of them are amazing. The ones in St John's Wood are mega! Five-star stuff. The people who live there are so rich, their throw outs have to be seen to be believed. Prada. Chanel. Dolce and Gabbana. Honest. In a charity shop! You'd have loved it, Nesta. And you too, Lucy. All those great designer clothes going so cheap. And I got a couple of books and CDs that I wanted for almost nothing.'

'Sounds like you've had a better morning than us. Need anyone to do any more research?' asked Izzie.

'Sure,' said TJ. 'We need someone to do North Finchley and Hampstead to see what's there. So far, seems St John's Wood is the biz for fashion, Muswell Hill for books, East Finchley for bric-à-brac.'

I couldn't help feeling a stab of envy. She's a clever girl, is TJ, and sometimes I feel a bit jealous of her. Looks and brains. She has the whole package. I wished I'd thought of something like that instead of breaking my back sorting through smelly clothes and making my friends suffer with me. Suddenly I had an idea.

I didn't want TJ to think we'd had a bad time when she'd been having a great time so I decided to pop back into the shop for a minute.

Once in there, I grabbed the pair of striped yellow and lime green tights and pulled them on. I looked around for some more mad things to wear and spotted the Afro wig, a pink ostrich feather boa and a pair of swimming goggles. I quickly put them on, then made a quick dash to the little toilet area to see what I looked like. I couldn't help but laugh when I saw my reflection in the mirror above the tiny sink. I looked truly awful. Like someone with the worse possible taste ever.

A moment later, I stepped back out into the street and my outfit had exactly the right effect. Lucy, TJ and Izzie creased up laughing when they saw me.

'You're a closet Nancy No-taste,' said Lucy. 'I always knew you would come out one day.'

I went into a dance routine like Mike Myers in the movie, *Austin Powers*, and the girls continued laughing and a few passers-by looked at me as if I was bonkers. See TJ, I thought, you're not the only one having fun doing charity work. After a few moments, Izzie began to shake her head and twitch her mouth. Cool, I thought, she's getting into it as well, and I began to shake my head and twitch as well as I revved up the manic dancing.

'No, *noooo*,' grimaced Izzie, twitching her mouth more than ever.

I began to strut up and down the pavement like a model who's had too much caffeine. 'Yeah, baby, yeah. Hey, Izzie. Love and peace. Like yeah, baby, yeaaah . . .'

Lucy had joined in the twitching with Izzie by now and was also making strange faces.

'St John's Wood may be good for the more expensive designs,' I said in a high pitched squeaky voice, 'but we all know that Muswell Hill is the most brilliant place for those individual little fashions that you won't find anywhere else.'

'Yeah, *right*,' drawled a familiar voice behind me.

I spun around and almost knocked William Lewis over.

'I was trying to warn you,' said Izzie as William looked me up and down with that infuriatingly amused look of his.

'Yeah,' he said with a wicked grin. 'Individual is the word but not so much Coco Chanel as Coco the Clown. Ever thought of getting some fashion advice from an expert?'

Fashion advice? Me? Queen of style? Hurumph. Luckily Izzie, TJ and Lucy pulled me back towards the shop before I could sock him in the mouth.

If you think you're too small to have an impact,
try going to bed with a mosquito.
Anita Roddick

Chapter 6

Jumble

'The cheek of him! Who does he think he is?' I asked after I'd changed back into my normal clothes in the tiny cloakroom in the shop. 'And anyway, he looks like *he* could do with some fashion advice. Those jeans are *so* yesterday. And did you see that T-shirt? Give me a break. Positively prehistoric.'

'You really do fancy him, don't you?' said Lucy with a smirk.

'For the millionth time I DO NOT fancy William Lewis.'

Izzie began smirking as well. Both of them were standing in front of me smirking like smirky things competing in a smirking contest. It was sooooooo annoying.

'Oh,' continued Lucy. 'So you won't want to know that it was him who came to collect the jumble.'

'Don't worry,' added Izzie. 'He's gone. He took it while you were in the Ladies changing out of your wig. He said to say he hoped to see you there.'

'Where?'

'At the jumble sale,' said Lucy. 'Keep up!'

'And did he say that he wanted to see me or us there?'

'What does it matter if you don't fancy him?' asked Izzie.

'It doesn't. I'm just asking.'

'He said he hoped he'd see *you*,' said Lucy. 'I reckon you're in with a chance there.'

'Like I care,' I said.

'What is it with him?' asked Izzie. 'Usually you'd be right in there. Cute boy to be conquered. He's sooooo your type, so what's the problem?'

'No problem. Just he's *not* my type. Honest, I really, really, really don't fancy him,' I said. 'He thinks he's so cool. And with that look of his, like he's always laughing at some private joke.'

'I like him,' said Lucy. 'He seems on the level to me.'

'Like as in fancy?'

Lucy shook her head. 'Like as in like.'

'She's still too wrapped up in your brother to fancy anyone else,' said Izzie.

'Pfff. Him,' I said, then sighed. 'One day you'll come to your senses. At least we can only hope that you will. What do you think of William, Izzie?'

'Yeah, he's OK . . .' she started.

'Actually, I don't care. I think he thinks a lot of himself. He's a smart-arse.'

'Hmmm,' said Lucy with a grin. 'That's what he said about you too.'

'He did?'

'Yeah. Just now when you were changing,' said Izzie.

'What a cheek!'

'He said it in a nice way. Like it was a good thing,' said Lucy.

'How did he say it? Say it *exactly* how he said it,' I insisted.

'He said, she's a bit of a smart-arse your mate isn't she?' said Lucy. 'And he said it with a knowing smirk, like he knew *your* type and found you entertaining. I think he thought your manic dancing was quite funny too.'

'God, he annoys me. I really hate him.'

Lucy and Izzie exchanged knowing looks.

'Yeah, sure,' said Izzie. 'You hate him.'

Lucy started laughing as though Izzie had said something really funny. Both of them are clearly demented. They exchanged glances and Izzie raised an eyebrow

'So are you going to go?' asked Lucy.

'Might,' I said. 'In fact, Mrs Owen did mention that they need volunteers tomorrow as well so yeah, I might go along to the jumble sale just to show him how I can look when I want to make an effort. When I'm not dressed as a cartoon character. Not because I fancy him or anything, because I don't, but because I don't like people telling me I need fashion advice when they don't really know me.'

Lucy and Izzie exchanged dubious glances as if to say that they didn't believe a word of it.

On Sunday morning, I spent a good hour trying to find the perfect outfit to wear to the jumble sale. It was a difficult decision and I was glad that Mum had made me keep some of the clothes I was about to chuck out or else I'd have had nothing to choose from. Usually I'm so good at those 'what to wear to where?' type quizzes in magazines. The ones that show you five outfits and five occasions and you have to match the outfit to the occasion. I get it right every time but a jumble sale wasn't an occasion that had ever come up. What should one wear? I didn't want to look too scruffy because I wanted to show William that I could look good, but then I didn't want to look like I'd tried too hard either. He might think I was trying to impress him. Casual but stylish, that's what I need, I decided. Something that looked like I'd thrown it on without thinking, but actually showed off all my best features to their best advantage.

I know, I thought as I scanned the shelves in my wardrobe. My retro lilac cardi, my scuffed bootleg jeans and my lilac Converse Allstar sneakers. A pink tie-dye camisole underneath and the zipper on my cardi pulled just low enough to see the lace on it and that should do the trick. Bit of make up. Not too much. Squirt of Mum's Ô de Lancome as it's light but feminine and he should be falling at my feet any time soon. Not that I want him to, that is, or, I do want him to, but only so that I can tell him that I don't want him to. Hmm, I thought. Sometimes I sound mixed up. But I'm not.

I met the girls at the church hall in Kilburn where the jumble sale was taking place and it seemed a shame that we were going to be indoors again as already it was warm and looked like it was going to be a lovely clear spring day. TJ was with us this time as she wanted to be a volunteer as well. She was looking very good with her hair loose and a bit of make-up on which is unusual for TJ, who often doesn't bother.

'If there are cute boys like William getting involved, I want to be a part of it,' she said after we'd been let in and Mrs Owen had given us instructions about how to lay out the stuff to be sold on the long tables lining the sides of the hall.

'Why? Do you fancy him?' I asked as casually as I could, as I began to pull bags out from under our allotted table on the right-hand side of the hall.

'Oh God no,' she said putting her hand on her heart. 'Scout's honour. On the Holy Bible. Truly, I'd say if I did. No. He's all yours, Nesta. There's no spark there between us. Honest. Not like . . .'

'Oh not you too, TJ. I *don't* fancy him.'

'Izzie and Lucy said you did.'

Lucy gave me a big smile from the front of the table from where she had begun arranging all the clothes by colour. I glared back at her.

'Well, I don't,' I insisted. 'I was just asking if *you* fancied him.'

'Well, I don't either.'

'Neither do I.'

'Yeah, but I'm telling the truth,' she said, smirking. She had obviously been taking smirking lessons from the current champions, Izzie and Lucy.

'Oh for heaven's sake. I DO NOT FANCY WILLIAM LEWIS!'

Izzie's face registered horror and Lucy began the twitching thing that she was doing yesterday. I spun round to see that

William had just walked in the door. He was carrying an enormous box of junk and he looked straight over to where we were and gave us a brief nod. He wasn't smiling as much as usual and I wasn't sure if he had heard what I'd said or not.

Huh, be like that, I thought as I watched him put down his box then head out again without even coming over to say hi. I know *his* type exactly. Charming when they want something then cool as ice when they don't. Not that I care either way.

The next few hours flew by. From the moment the doors opened to the public at ten o'clock, we were kept really busy. Lucy was in her element and set herself up as a style guru giving fashion advice to loads of the people who came to our table.

'Oh no,' she said to one grey haired lady who had picked up a burgundy coloured cardigan. 'Not your colour. I've got one just perfect for you tucked away, let me get it.'

Soon there were more people round our table than anyone's, all asking Lucy for advice. Not to be left out, Izzie began auctioning some stuff off. It was a riot as she held up a skirt.

'Ladies, ladies, bargain of the week,' she called into the room. 'A Jaeger skirt. Yes, the genuine article in perfect condition. None of your fake stuff here, only the best designer gear. What am I bid? We're starting at fifty pence. Does anyone raise me? Ah yes, sixty pence in the corner . . .'

We were a good team and the money started coming in fast. Before I knew it, it was twelve o'clock. I'd been so distracted with the auction that I hadn't noticed the girl sitting behind the table on the opposite side of the hall who was watching us with a smile on her face. She had white blond hair tied back, showing a stunningly pretty face. And she looked familiar. A few minutes later, the hall door opened and William went over to her and handed her a bottle of juice.

Huh, I thought. I knew there'd be a girl involved. I looked around for Lucy so I could tell her and saw her heading towards the cloakroom at the back of the hall. As TJ and Izzie were still busy with the auction which was proving a great success, I followed Lucy. I needed to tell someone that I'd been right about William.

'I *knew* it,' I said as I burst into the cloakroom.

'Knew what?' asked Lucy from the sink where she had started washing her hands.

'William's out there with a girl. I told you so. He isn't Mr Super Do Gooder. He's doing volunteer work to be with this girl. And she's *very* pretty.'

'So what's wrong with that?' asked Lucy. 'You heard TJ saying part of the reason she's here is to meet cute boys like William. But not William. I don't think she fancies him. Between you and me, I think part of her thought that Luke might be here. I don't think she ever really got over him, you know . . .'

'Oh who cares about Luke. It's William I'm talking about . . .'

'But you don't care about him,' said Lucy. 'Earlier you announced to the whole hall that you don't fancy him? Or *do* you? And anyway, what's wrong with doing some charity work to be with someone? You don't have to be a saint to do it. I'm sure people get involved for all sorts of reasons. As long as the work gets done, that's what counts in the end.'

'I guess,' I said and went back to the door and half opened it ready to go back into the hall. 'It's just – he could have found a better way to impress her.'

'Who?' asked Lucy.

'William Lewis. God, Lucy, anyone would think that you're not listening. There's just something about him that I don't trust.'

'Maybe that's because he's a friend of Luke's and you know that you can't trust him after what happened last year.'

'Maybe,' I said. 'I don't know what it is about him but somehow . . . he *annoys* me. And if he only got involved with this volunteer lark to impress that girl then I think he's sad.'

'Maybe *she* got involved to be with him,' said Lucy.

'Maybe,' I said. 'Anyway, whatever. He's annoying so I'm not going to give him even another moment's thought.'

I opened the door properly to go back into the hall and who was standing in the corridor waiting to come into the cloakroom. William freaking Lewis.

'Oh God, *you* again,' I blurted before I could stop myself. It seemed that every time I turned round lately he was there.

'Well pardon *me* for breathing,' he said.

'This is the Ladies,' I said.

'I think you'll find that it's the Anybody's,' he said. 'There's only one so it's the Ladies *and* the Gents.'

'Oh. Right. Whatever. How long were you standing there?'

William leant slightly towards me and I caught the scent of his aftershave. It was nice. Light and citrus. 'Long enough,' he said, 'to know that I am annoying.'

Oh God, I thought. I've really blown my cool now. He

overhears me twice in one day. Talk about unlucky.

'Right. Sorry. Got to go. Previous engagement,' I said as I made a dash back into the hall.

Buggero, buggera, buggerat, I thought as I made my way back to the table. I felt all mixed up. But why? What was going on with me? Did I secretly fancy William a bit? So secretly that not even I knew about it? No. That's mad. But then I am mad. And I'd be mad not to fancy him as he has got gorgeous eyes and he smells nice. Maybe we'd just got off to the wrong start. Anyway, it's too late. He's got a girlfriend. And she's gorgeous even though she looks slightly older than him. Do I mind? Nah. Yeah. Maybe. Oh I don't know. I'll think about it later. In the meantime, I have things to do. Bric-à-brac to sell. God, I wish I could scream but then people really would think I was barmy.

'Need more stuff out?' I asked when I got back to the others.

Izzie nodded. 'There are loads more boxes under the table. Be great if you could get some of it out. Thanks. You could hand it up to me.'

I knelt on the floor and swivelled myself under the table and began to pull out the contents of the boxes and hand them to Izzie. It was nice to be down there and out of the way for a while. I think I'm better off not being let out in public at the moment, I thought as I surveyed the room from my strange vantage point. All I could see of people were their lower legs and shoes. Five minutes later, a pair of jeans and trainers appeared on the other side of the table. And a wheelchair. William's legs, I thought. I recognise the trainers. I tugged the hem of Izzie's jeans and shook my head so that she'd know not to let him know that I was under there.

It wasn't much use as a moment later, William's face appeared under the table as he bent down.

'Hiding from anyone I know?' he asked.

'I wasn't hiding,' I said curtly as I crawled out and stood up. I was about to say something cutting but buttoned it when I saw that he was with the pretty girl from the other side of the hall and she was in the wheelchair. 'And certainly not from . . .'

'Eleanor,' said William to the girl before I could finish, 'I'd like you to meet – er, what was your name again?' And he gave me an infuriating smile.

'Nesta,' I said to the girl. 'Hi.'

'And we're Izzie, Lucy and TJ,' chorused the others from the other end of the table.

I looked at William. Same high cheekbones, fine features. The penny dropped. Eleanor. Oh!

'William's sister?' I asked.

Eleanor nodded. 'Yep. That's me.'

'But you . . . you look familiar,' I said. 'Have we met before?'

'Before this you mean?' asked Eleanor indicating the wheelchair she was in.

'Um, yes, no. I meant before today.'

'Don't think so,' said Eleanor.

'She might have seen you on stage,' said William.

'That's it,' Izzie interrupted. 'You're Eleanor Lewis. I saw you at Jackson's Lane. You were totally brilliant. Remember, Nesta? *The Snow Queen?*'

'God, yeah. You were amazing.' It had been a Christmas performance of the ballet and Eleanor had danced the main role. I remembered her because not only was she stunningly pretty but her dancing had something special. I remembered thinking that she had the X factor and the write-ups in the local paper had thought the same, some even comparing her to Sylvie Guillem, who I think is the best dancer in the whole world. Eleanor was in the press for a while and then suddenly seemed to disappear.

'What happened?' I asked, presuming that she'd broken a leg or sprained an ankle while dancing or something.

'Nesta,' said Lucy. 'Maybe it's private. Excuse our friend, Eleanor. We call her Big Mouth.'

'S'OK,' said Eleanor. 'She can ask. I got cancer.'

'You *what*?' I think my jaw dropped open. She just came out with it in such a matter of fact way, like she was telling us she had a sore throat or a sprained wrist.

'Cancer. In the bones,' she said and she looked at me straight in the eyes as if to see if I was going to look away.

'God, how awful,' I said looking straight back at her. 'Are you going to be all right? Can it be treated?'

The others looked surprised but I really wanted to know.

Eleanor shook her head. 'No. They've done what they can. Nothing left to try.'

'But that's so unfair . . .' I blurted.

She shrugged and looked up at her brother. 'Tell me about it. Yeah, but at least I can get my brother to do anything for me now, huh, Will?'

William nodded. 'Just about.'

'One of the good things about everyone knowing that you're going to die is that no one can refuse you anything. Now when I go shopping, I can have whatever I want . . .'

'You're going to *die*?' I asked and turned to William. I had a feeling that I was reacting in completely the wrong way but I was so shocked. I couldn't help it.

William put his hand on Eleanor's shoulder and smiled at her but I saw the pain in his eyes.

'Yeah. Bummer, huh?' said Eleanor. 'Still, so are we all. It's just I know that my time's coming a bit before most.'

'I'm *so* sorry,' I said. 'And I hope I didn't offend you, just I've never met anyone with cancer before and they don't teach us the "how to deal with a person who's got cancer" lesson at school.'

'Hey Nesta, don't worry,' she said. 'Actually I like the fact that you came out and asked what you wanted to know. Some people, even those I thought were my friends, cross the road when they see me now. Can't deal with it. Hah. How do they think *I* feel? So it's refreshing when someone comes out with the questions that I know they're dying to ask . . . Dying to ask — there's a funny one.'

Just at that moment, William was called away by one of the ladies running the sale.

'Won't be long,' he said to Eleanor then turned to me. 'Keep an eye on her, will you?'

'Sure,' I said.

Eleanor looked at her wheelchair and held up her hands in

exasperation. 'Like there's anything I could get up to in this thing. Give me a break, Will, I'm fine.'

'Is there anything I can do?' I asked when he'd gone.

Eleanor looked at me then over at her brother. Then her expression took on the same amused look that I'd seen on William's face sometimes

'Yeah,' she said. 'Cheer my misery of a brother up. He's been a pain in the ass for months now. Anyone would think it was him that was ill.'

'What! *Me*? *Him*? I . . . er, I don't think he likes me very much.'

'I wouldn't be so sure,' said Eleanor.

'No. I am sure.'

Eleanor shrugged. 'Well you did ask what you could do. I saw him watching you before and I . . . well I just have an instinct that you two would get along.'

'Pff. Doubt it but OK. OK. I'll try,' I said.

'Cool,' said Eleanor. 'Just don't let him know I asked you will you?'

Izzie, TJ and Lucy gave me the thumbs up from the other end of the table from where they'd all been listening to every word.

Cheer William up. Now *that* was going to be a challenge.

William

'So now we know why he got involved in doing all this kind of thing,' said TJ after William and Eleanor had gone.

The morning rush had faded and the hall had grown quiet. I felt all mixed up inside and judging by the looks on the other's faces, the general mood was gloom. I was beginning to wish that I'd never got involved in doing volunteer work. It stirred up too many weird feelings and made me think about stuff I wasn't sure I wanted to. Illness, death. I felt so helpless.

'I just can't believe it,' said Izzie. 'Eleanor Lewis. She's so beautiful . . .'

'Beautiful people get ill too,' said Lucy.

'But to know that you're going to die so young, I can't imagine it,' I said.

'It seems so unfair. She had such a brilliant future,' said Izzie.

'So does anyone who gets ill at her age,' said TJ. 'She's what? Seventeen, eighteen?'

'Just turned nineteen,' said Mrs Owen who had been quietly

sitting at one end of the table listening. 'She's been through a lot that one. She's a brave girl.'

'Do you know the family?' I asked

Mrs Owen nodded. 'I've known William, Olivia and Eleanor all their lives. I live on the same street and used to babysit them when they were young.'

'So what's going to happen to her?' I asked. 'I mean, how long has she got?'

'A year. Maybe two,' replied Mrs Owen. 'You can never tell. Sometimes it's very quick and sometimes people outlive all expectations.'

Poor, poor Eleanor, I thought. Poor, poor William. Poor Olivia. And their mum and dad. What must his parents be going through? I wondered.

'This is what this is all about,' said Mrs Owen, indicating the hall with a sweep of her hands. 'These jumble sales, the shop. All the money goes to help the younger people with terminal cancer.'

'Help them how?' I asked. 'Eleanor said that there was no more anyone could do.'

'We can make them as comfortable as possible when they have to go through their treatment and . . . and at the end. All the proceeds of this sale will go to the Lotus Hospice.'

'Is that like a special hospital?' asked Lucy.

Mrs Owen nodded. 'It certainly has all the equipment needed there and the drugs for pain relief like a hospital but it's more than that. We try to make it as much like home as possible so that in their last weeks or days, they don't feel like they're in a hospital ward. They can get the care and medical attention they need but they can also have their family around them should they wish, eat together, spend time together. That's the aim. A small wing with a kitchen, a living area and spare beds so that family or friends can stay over and they can bring in all their things – books, posters, whatever, and make it their own for their time there. William's been a star and so has Olivia. Both of them have worked harder than anyone to raise funds because although we have one living area like that, we need another – sometimes more than one family has a need for the place at the same time. It can be so hard for family members to stand by and know that there's nothing that they can do to save their loved one. At least with this, William can feel he is doing something.'

And I'd accused him of doing it to pull girls. And he'd probably heard. He must think that I am the worst person in the world.

'There's nothing else for it,' I said turning to Lucy. 'I have to apologise to William.'

Lucy nodded. 'I think you should. And you have to cheer him up. Eleanor said so.'

'Do you know if William will be back today?' I asked Mrs Owen.

'Later,' she replied. 'He's gone to drop Eleanor home and then he'll be back.'

Right, I thought. Apologise and commence Mission Cheer Up William. How in the world was I going to do that? I had no idea. I tried to put myself in his shoes and imagine that it was Tony who was ill, or one of my mates. I don't think I could bear it, I thought as my eyes filled with tears at the very idea of anything happening to any of them.

Mrs Owen noticed my long face. 'Hey come on, Nesta. No use in you getting all gloomy. It doesn't help. My old dad always used to say that the birds of doom may fly overhead but there's no need to let them nest in your hair. He was right. So. You know what you can do? Be happy. Enjoy your life to the best of your ability.'

'It's weird. Why are some people so well and have everything whilst others have such a hard time?'

'Big question,' said Mrs Owen. 'Which is exactly why you should enjoy your life while you *are* well. All of it. Including all the trivialities of life. Be glad that you can.'

I nodded back at her, and attempted a smile.

Then the afternoon bargain hunters appeared through the doors, including one face that was very familiar. It was Miss Watkins, our PSHE teacher. No surprise there, I thought as she began to sift through one of the tables by the door. She always looks as if she dressed from the jumble in mismatched outfits that don't really suit her. She's a funny old bird. Strict as hell when she wants to be, but supportive and kind when she sees someone making an effort. Shame she doesn't make an effort with her appearance. She has that wiry grey hair that seems to have a life of its own but I'm sure could look halfway decent if she had it blow dried. And she wears really old-fashioned glasses that make her look permanently shocked.

'Oh well done, girls,' she said coming over after she'd had a good browse round. 'So good to see some of our pupils here. How's it going?'

'Good,' said Lucy.

'Yes, in fact Lucy's set herself up as a style queen,' I interrupted. 'She could recommend a whole new image for you if you like.'

Lucy looked at me as if she'd like to kill me but I thought it was a brilliant idea.

'New image? Me? Oh no, I'm quite happy,' said Miss Watkins, causing Lucy to sigh with relief. Wacko Watkins has never been her favourite teacher.

'And we were just saying that we thought that our school should do some fundraising,' said TJ.

Miss Watkins chortled. 'What planet are you on, Theresa Watts?' she asked. 'We do. Of course we do.'

'No, we mean for charities,' continued Lucy. 'We know we do loads of fundraising for the school . . .'

'But we *do*,' Miss Watkins repeated. 'And this is one of the main charities we support.'

'Really?' said Izzie. 'How come we never knew about it?'

Miss Watkins gave us all her 'how stupid can you get look' (a look that she has clearly perfected through the years). 'How come you never knew about it? Hmm. Maybe you weren't listening. People often only hear what they want to hear. But oh yes, we do fundraising. Not that we couldn't do a lot more. The meeting is on Monday nights after school. You're all very welcome as we could do with some fresh blood.'

Lucy, Izzie, TJ and I looked at each other then we all nodded.

'We're in,' said TJ.

'Excellent,' said Miss Watkins. 'Now. What bargains have you got to show me?'

William came back at about two-thirty just as all the volunteers were beginning to pack up. He came straight over to me and pulled me to one side.

'Thanks for . . . before, with Eleanor,' he said. 'She said she really appreciated being talked to like a normal human being for change. It really is true what she said before – about people not knowing how to deal with her so they avoid her or the subject of her illness. They talk about anything else but what's happening.'

'But it must be so hard,' I replied, 'for you too. If there's anything I can do or if you want to talk . . .'

William's expression grew hard for a moment. 'Eleanor may want to talk, but not me. No. Last thing I want,' he said. 'What good would that do? Like there's anything you could say to make it better.'

He looked so intense and I remembered that I was supposed to be cheering him up. I quickly scanned my brain for something I could say to help.

'I could try and say something to make you laugh . . .'

'Don't bother.'

'Look. I'm really really sorry about . . . um, whatever I said before. About you being . . . um annoying and stuff . . .'

'Doesn't matter,' said William. 'I probably am.'

He looked so sad as he stood there. Like a little boy who

was desperately trying to be brave. He needed distracting. And fast.

'Er . . . OK,' I said and pointed to the back of the church hall. 'See that screen over there?'

'Yeah.'

'Come behind it with me and I'll snog you.'

William burst out laughing.

'See,' I said. 'I told you I could make you laugh.'

The amused look that had been annoying me so much lately appeared back on his face. 'Ah . . . but did you mean it?' he asked.

Time for a little practice flirting, I thought and glanced back at him in a coy way. 'Why? Do you want me to have meant it?'

'Depends. Do you want me to take you up on it?'

I looked at his mouth. It was a very nice mouth, wide with a bottom lip that plumped out in the middle like a tiny soft cushion. I glanced up into his eyes and a shiver of anticipation went through me. For a moment, it was as if we were locked together. Suddenly he grabbed my hand. We quickly walked over behind the screen where we were out of sight and he pulled me close to him and kissed me. Properly. Like, not a peck. I mean, *properly*. Then we pulled apart and both burst out laughing.

'Better than talking,' he said, grinning.

'Right,' I said. 'Yes. Good.' I felt weak at the knees from the kiss. I hadn't imagined for a moment that he would take me up on my offer. I'd said it to make him laugh. His response had taken me unexpectedly and on the kissing scale, he was a ten out of ten.

He gazed into my eyes and I felt myself turning to jelly. He pulled me close again and once more, we kissed. I could have stayed there forever if we hadn't heard Izzie and Lucy sniggering a short distance away. I opened my eyes.

They were doing that smirking thing again.

The birds of doom may fly overhead
but there's no need to let them nest in your hair.

Chapter 8

Fundraising

'Oh no. Look who's in there,' I groaned as I looked through the window of the prefab where the fundraising meeting was being held after school on Monday. I could see four prefects from Year Eleven waiting for the meeting to begin. Doreen Kennard, Blair Thorpe, Charlotte Miller and Sandra Collins.

'Who?' asked Lucy.

'Dopey Doreen and her sad bossy mates.'

'Don't be so cruel, Nesta,' said Lucy. 'You wouldn't like it if someone said that about you.'

'Yeah, but I didn't come up with that name. Everyone calls them that,' I said. 'They are so boring. Remember when Blair gave that talk in assembly last year? I can't even remember what it was about. I was asleep after five minutes.'

'It was about drugs,' said Izzie.

'None of which could possibly be as potent as her speaking voice,' I said. 'One of the most powerful tranquillisers I've ever come across.'

TJ and Izzie laughed but Lucy punched my arm.

'Come on. Let's do a runner now,' I said. 'We'll find another way to do something . . . like donating our organs when we're dead.'

'*Nesta*,' groaned Lucy. 'Gross.'

'Well, they're no use to you when you're six foot under are they? I mean, I know I'm Queen of Squeam now I'm alive but when I'm dead, anyone can have anything. Like if any of you girls want a kidney or whatever, please feel free.'

'Wow, thanks Nesta,' said TJ. 'I'd love a kidney. I could have it bottled and put on the mantelpiece as a reminder of you.'

'And I'll have your eyeballs,' said Izzie, laughing. 'I could have them made into earrings.'

Lucy put her fingers in her ears. '*Stop* it. You're all *disgusting*.'

'Oops. Too late to do a runner,' said Izzie suddenly putting a straight face on. 'Here comes Wacko.'

I turned to see Miss Watkins approaching. She was wearing a long, navy-coloured cardigan that she'd bought at the sale yesterday and her face lit up when she saw us.

'Well done, girls,' she said. 'I was hoping you lot would turn up. Come on then, let's get inside.'

Five minutes later, the meeting was underway and Miss Watkins asked Boring Blair to fill us 'new girls' in on forthcoming events.

I had a hard time not falling asleep again much as I tried to concentrate on what Blair was saying. It was something about the tone of her voice. Or lack of tone. She spoke every word on the same level. She wouldn't last five seconds on the radio.

I tried to focus once more and told myself that Blair's lack of delivery didn't matter as everyone knows she wants to be a marine biologist when she leaves school. Poor fish. The fishermen won't need nets. They can just send Blair underwater and ask her to say something and the fish will all surrender in droves. In fact maybe she is perfect for the job of fundraiser – she could hypnotise people into giving their money away. I almost laughed as an image of thousands of people walking down the road like sleepwalkers and handing over thousands of pounds to Blair played through my mind. 'Sleep sleep, hand over your cash,' she said in my fantasy.

'Nesta,' said Miss Watkins. 'What are you smiling at?'

'Smiling? Me? Oh. Yes, Miss. Just thinking about fundraising ideas.'

'Want to share those thoughts? That's what the meeting is all about. Sharing ideas.'

'Er no, Miss. Thank you. Not yet. Thank you.'

Somehow I didn't think my fantasy of Blair as Queen of the Zombies was an idea that would go down that well in the present company. Doreen, Blair and their mates are a peculiar lot. Although people call them the Dopey Doreens, actually they are all dead clever. They're not exactly pretty girls but they're not unattractive either. Somewhere in the middle and all of them look like they go to very expensive hairdressers, in fact Charlotte has the glossiest auburn hair I've ever seen even though it is a little thin. Doreen's small and brunette. Charlotte tall and skinny. Blair is tall with a mane of blond hair. And Sandra's medium-sized with wild, curly, dark hair. So pretty normal in the main. The thing about them is that they're . . . what is it? I thought as I searched my mind for the right word.

They're always up for awards for this and that. Mainly to do with science. Clever? No. Responsible? That's partly the word, as they have always been the prefect type. No. I know the word. Adult. It's like they somehow skipped childhood and adolescence and went straight into being grown up. Maybe they were even *born* grown up. I could feel myself smiling again as I imagined them in a play school reading books whilst around them other kids played with toys.

'Nesta, *Nesta*,' said Miss Watkins. 'You're daydreaming again. Come on. Join in. That's why you're here.'

'OK. So how much has been raised so far?' I asked.

'Two hundred and fifty pounds,' said Blair looking pleased with herself.

'And how much is needed to build the new wing at the Lotus Hospice?' I asked.

'Well, that's among other things,' said Sandra. 'We support a number of charities.'

'Yes, but we agreed that the hospice would be our focus for the first half of the year,' said Miss Watkins. 'They have a target that they are trying to reach and all the schools in this area did promise that we would make them our priority until the sum has been raised.'

'And the sum is?' I asked.

'Another fifty thousand pounds is needed,' said Miss Watkins. 'And they were hoping to get it by the beginning of May so the building could commence later on in the month.'

Doreen laughed. 'Unlikely,' she said.

'Not possible,' said Charlotte.

'Thanks to some very generous benefactors, four hundred thousand has been raised by various organisations so far,' said Miss Watkins, 'but all those sources have now been exhausted, so it's down to creativity and hard graft from now on. Just to make that last amount needed.'

The Dopey Doreens were all shaking their heads.

'But why not?' I asked.

Sandra gave me a very snooty look. 'Have you actually done any fundraising?' she asked.

'Yes,' I answered. So I'd only done yesterday's jumble sale, but she didn't need to know that.

'Then you'll know exactly how hard it is to extract money out of people,' Sandra continued. 'At least, enough to make a difference.'

'And you wouldn't believe how many people pitch up like you lot, full of enthusiasm, only to drop out a few weeks later when they realise what hard work it is,' said Blair and the others nodded along with her.

'Doesn't need to be hard work,' I blurted. 'Well, OK, maybe a bit of graft but I don't see why it can't be enjoyable as well.' I was thinking of the auction we'd had yesterday and what a laugh that had been for all of us. Volunteers and buyers.

'Yeah right,' drawled Doreen in a tired way. 'Just what we need. Another naïve idealist.'

'Now come on,' said Miss Watkins. 'You don't want to put off our new arrivals on their first night.'

Doreen gave her a look back which said, that's exactly what I want to do. I got a feeling that this fundraising thing was their little club and they didn't want outsiders in. It was no wonder others had dropped out so quickly. When faced with this lot, I thought, who could blame them? But I wasn't about to do a runner. I like a challenge and I don't like people insinuating that I can't do something. Huh, I thought. I'd show them who the naïve idealist really was.

'OK then,' I said. 'So what's on the agenda? More jumble sales? Raffles? What?'

'The big event in the calendar year is the dance on May 7th,' said Miss Watkins. 'How's that going Blair?'

'Well, we've got the venue,' said Blair.

'Which is where?' asked TJ.

'It's a hall in East Finchley at the end of the High Road . . .'

'Oh, I know it,' said Izzie, then pulled a disapproving face. 'It's where I . . . er . . . It's a bit dark and stuffy in there.'

I knew the hall too. It was where Izzie went to a slimming club called Weight Winners but she obviously didn't want the others knowing how she knew the place.

'So you find somewhere on no budget,' challenged Charlotte. 'We can brighten it up on the night with a few balloons.'

Izzie caught my eye. I knew she thinking the same thing that I was: Sounds like the party of the century. Not.

'And how are the ticket sales going?' asked Miss Watkins.

At this question, Blair looked down at the floor, faintly embarrassed. 'Ah. Not brilliant so far . . .'

'How many?' asked Miss Watkins.

'Twenty-five. Sorry. I . . . Look, we've got time yet.'

'Five weeks,' said Miss Watkins. 'Five weeks and we need to

sell at least five hundred. The hall will easily take that number, and even more at a push.'

'Have you advertised it?' asked TJ. 'I could put it in the school magazine for a start. I certainly didn't know that there was going to be any event in May, and if people don't know about it, no one's going to buy tickets.'

'Yeah. Have you got any posters out there?' asked Izzie.

Charlotte pulled a pile of posters out of her bag and held them up. They were black and white and showed little sense of design, in fact they looked like newspaper cuttings.

'I've put these up in a few of the libraries,' she said.

For girls with brains, this lot aren't that bright, I thought – but then it was always the same in every year: the ones who did well academically weren't always the most sussed when it came to street cred or doing anything commercial.

After looking at the posters, I glanced over at Lucy and pulled a 'God they're awful face'.

Unfortunately Blair saw me. 'OK then, let's see you lot do better,' she said. 'Charlotte spent ages doing those. Honestly Miss Watkins. Do we have to work with this lot from Year Ten?'

Miss Watkins' eyes were twinkling as if she was secretly enjoying what was going on. 'Team effort, girls,' she said. 'Team effort. Now have you new girls got any suggestions that you'd like to throw into the pot?'

I nodded. I was sure that Lucy, Izzie, TJ and I could raise more than two hundred and fifty pounds if we put our heads together. Sir Bob raised millions for Ethiopia in one night, so what was fifty thousand?

'Give us a few days,' I said. 'We'll come up with some ideas.'

'Well, don't do anything stupid,' said Doreen. 'And make sure that you consult us before starting. We're experienced and know what we're doing.'

'Which is why you raised the grand sum of two hundred and fifty quid,' I said as Lucy, Izzie and TJ gasped in horror.

Doreen looked as if she'd like to thump me and Blair, Sandra and Charlotte scowled at all of us with undisguised disdain. Now I knew that we had definitely stamped on their territory. Not that Miss Watkins seemed bothered by any of the animosity taking place in front of her. She was still smiling away as if at some private joke. Well tough to the lot of you, I thought as I met Doreen's glare in an eyeball to eyeball staring contest. You're not getting rid of us this easily.

Doreen looked away and murmured, 'So childish.'

I didn't care what she thought. I'd made up my mind that I wanted to do something for the Lotus Hospice and she wasn't going to get in the way. It was because of something that TJ had said. It was at the jumble sale and made things click into place for me. She'd said, 'I suppose for most people, people in need are all so far away and it doesn't seem real. The people are anonymous but then when something affects someone close to you and you put a face and a family to a tragedy or disaster, then it all becomes so real.'

I nodded. That's was how I felt now having met Eleanor. She was real and I couldn't help but feel that it might have been me in her place or someone that I knew. The Lotus Hospice was my chosen charity now and I meant to give it my best.

Chapter 9

Diamond
Destiny

'We need a good theme for the dance,' said Lucy in the lunch break at school the next day.

'Yeah,' I agreed. 'It definitely needs something. I couldn't believe those posters. *A dance. The first Saturday in May*. Like, so what? How dull is that? Wouldn't attract me to go. It has to be like an event. Something you feel you can't miss out on. A happening type of happening.'

'Exactly,' said Lucy. 'Which is why we need a theme.'

'But what?' asked TJ.

'Don't know,' said Lucy. 'But we need to give people an excuse to dress up. I think people like that, least I know I do.'

'Yeah, speak for yourself,' said TJ. 'I'm happy in my jeans and T-shirt. How about we do a barn dance sort of thing.'

'Not glam enough. Who wants to dance about with a bit of straw stuck between their teeth?' said Izzie.

'Sounds OK to me,' said TJ.

'You have much to learn about being cool my dumb little chum,' I said.

'So what can our theme be?' asked Izzie. 'All in red, all in gold, all in silver?'

'Cowboys and Indians. Vicars and tarts. Hollywood,' suggested Lucy.

'I think we should write down an A–Z of themes,' said TJ. 'Be useful for when one of us throws a party in the future, as well as for the dance. Plus, it would be great to put in the mag as a feature. In fact, it would be cool to do a whole section on parties.'

We spent the next fifteen minutes trying to think up themes and although some of them were really good, none of them felt right for the dance.

'Some people hate dressing up,' I said. 'And it might put them off coming if they think they've got to hire a fancy dress costume. No. All in silver or all in white or something like that is more do-able and won't cost a lot but . . . I don't know. As Izzie said, it just needs to be more glam, I think.'

'I know,' said Lucy. 'As I said, a chance to dress up, that's it. A chance to put on your bling and strut your stuff. How about something like the Bling Ball?'

'Yeah, great idea,' said Izzie. 'But not sure about the name. Sounds a bit downmarket. We need to sell a lot of tickets to fill the place and get some atmosphere going.'

'But even if we sell a load of tickets,' said TJ, 'at only eight quid each, we still need to do something else to raise fifty thousand. I had a look on the Net last night and found a few sites with some really good ideas.'

'And I've had a few ideas,' said Lucy.

'Me too,' said Izzie.

'So let's hear them,' I said. 'Let's brainstorm.' I'd heard my dad use this term a million times when sitting round the table at home working on film ideas with his various producers.

We spent the next half hour writing down everything we could come up with for Miss Watkins and the Dopey Doreens. Soon we had a good list with suggestions from the insane to the sensible.

'So what have we got so far chairperson?' I asked TJ as she had been the one writing everything down.

TJ began to read from her list: 'Sponsored skydiving . . .'

'Bit risky,' said Izzie. 'Although we could suggest our teachers do it. Bet we'd raise a fortune!'

'Sponsored walks or marathons – bit more sensible,' continued TJ, 'raffles, home services, cleaning, mowing lawns, taking care of pets . . .'

'Oh, add car washing,' said Lucy. 'That wouldn't be hard to do.'

'And if you offer to do it naked apart from a daffodil up your bum, you could charge double,' I said.

'Oh get serious, Nesta,' said Izzie. 'Not a daffodil. No. I see Lucy with a tulip.'

TJ ignored Izzie and I and continued with the list. 'A swim-a-thon. A games night. Candle-making. Competitions like guess the name of a teacher, guess the number of coins in a jar. Face painting.'

'I've got a brilliant one,' I interrupted as an idea flashed into my head. 'A calendar. Your brother could shoot it Lucy. We could be like the women in that movie *Calendar Girls*.'

'What, as in naked? Miss Watkins would never allow it,' Lucy replied.

'She can be in it as well . . .'

'*Eeeewww*,' chorused TJ, Lucy and Izzie.

'In fact, all the teachers could be in it,' I said. 'Imagine Mr Johnson as Mr November lying over the desk . . .'

Lucy and Izzie cracked up.

'*Double* eeeewwww,' said TJ. 'You really are fixated on people being naked to raise money. But I'll put it down on the list and we can finalise things later. So, what else can we do – hopefully with our clothes on? Sports tournaments – that would give us a good chance to get loads of boys involved. Art sale. Gardening. Dog-walking – oh, got that one already. Recipe books with people's faves in. Quiz nights. Carrying groceries for people. Spelling competitions. Book sales. A football goal shoot-out . . .'

'How about a crèche for mothers who can never go shopping?' asked Izzie. 'We look after their kids for a couple of hours.'

'I'll put it on the list,' said TJ scribbling it down.

'And how about a kiss for a pound,' suggested Lucy.

'But you never know who might pay up to snog,' I said. 'You might end up kissing someone you don't like.'

Izzie got a cheeky look on her face. 'Oh you mean like you and William on Sunday?'

'I did that because Eleanor asked me to,' I said.

'She asked you to cheer him up,' said Lucy. 'Not stick your tongue down his throat.'

Of course we'd already discussed the William situation. As soon as he'd gone on Sunday, in fact. The girls had been gobsmacked to find us in an Oscar award-winning smooch at the back of the hall. My excuse to them was that it was my way of apologising and that I hadn't changed my mind about the way I felt about him. None of them bought it, and they all regard me with suspicion whenever I mention him so I decided to come clean and admit that maybe I do like him a little. Or maybe a lot as after the jumble sale I couldn't stop replaying the moment he'd grabbed me and pulled me towards him. It was *so* Rhett Butler and Scarlet in *Gone With the Wind*.

'I'm making up my mind about him,' I said.

'Looks like it's already made up to me,' said Lucy.

'Exactly,' said Izzie and TJ.

'No . . .'

'Why are you holding back with him?' asked Izzie. 'It's so clear that you like him.'

I had to admit I'd been asking that question myself and the answer was beginning to dawn on me. It was fear. Fear of being rejected. Fear of being hurt. Everyone always thinks I'm the confident one. The one who knows about boys but actually my track record isn't as brilliant as I make out. My last boyfriend Luke turned out to be two-timing me with one of my best friends and God knows how many others I don't know about. And before him, there was Simon and he dumped me. Not because he didn't like me any more but because he was going to

University in Scotland and didn't want to do the long distance thing. Still, it hurt. And then along comes William. Prince Cutenik himself but I don't want to open myself up to get hurt again. I want to be sure before I get involved again. Plus the fact that I haven't been practising what I preach. I always tell the girls, don't be too easy, play hard to get a bit. I didn't with Simon, I fell into his lap, literally as we met on a train and it lurched and there I was in his arms. And with Luke, we met and were soon an item. No, I wanted to take things with William a lot, *lot* slower.

A moment later, my mobile rang and I moved off to answer it. It was William. I went into the corridor outside the dining hall to talk to him without the others listening in and making stupid faces at me when they realised who it was.

'Oh, hi,' I said trying to sound as cool as I could. I still wasn't sure what to make of what had happened on Sunday. The kissing session had been very enjoyable (*very*) and for a few moments had completely swept me off my feet but then later, after he'd gone, that was when I began to worry that it had all happened too fast. I mean, we hadn't even been out on a date and already we'd done the lip lock. And in public. He might think I was way too easy and I didn't want that. Plus there was still the fact that he was a mate of Luke's so was he to be trusted? I felt I needed to back off a bit and just cheer him up as his sister had asked. Bake him a cake or something equally innocent.

'Hi yourself,' he said.

'So what can I do for you?' I asked.

'Yes. About Sunday . . .'

'Yes,' I said. 'Sorry. Don't know what came over me. Sorry. Won't happen again.'

'Oh,' he said and in that one word I could hear that he was disappointed. 'I was hoping that maybe we could get together for a repeat performance some time.'

'Yes. Well – about that . . .'

'What?'

I decided to take the plunge and tell him what was bothering me. 'See. Thing is William . . . you know I went out with Luke for a while?'

'Yes.'

'It makes things complicated.'

'Why? You're not going out with him any more.'

'True, but . . .'

'It's OK, Nesta. I get it. Never mind.'

'No. I don't think you do. Listen. Just he . . . um . . . it turned out I couldn't trust him.'

I heard William chuckle at the other end of the phone. 'Yeah. He does have a bit of a reputation.'

'And you're his mate.'

There was a silence for a few moments and I think the penny dropped. 'Ah. So you think that I might be the same?'

'Yes. How do I know that you're not?'

'You don't,' he said.

'Which makes it difficult.'

'So try me.'

I was beginning to feel that I was being a bit unfair on him and hearing his voice again made me remember how toe-curling the kiss had felt. It would be a shame to let it all go by just because his mate was a rat.

'So, what do you reckon?' William persisted. 'Want to go out sometime? I can probably fit you in between all my other lovers.'

'Yeah, very funny. Actually I was wondering if I could fit *you* in between all my other lovers.'

'Maybe it's just not destined to be,' said William in a sad voice but I had a feeling that he was joshing. 'But then we have seen each other twice over the last week after not seeing each other for months. Maybe it's destiny bringing us together.'

'Ah yes, destiny. Sometimes you can't fight it,' I said in an actressy-type voice.

'And by the way, Eleanor said hi. She liked meeting you.'

'I liked meeting her.' I didn't want to ask any more about her as he had made it clear on Sunday that he didn't want to talk about the situation and if there's one thing I know about boys, it's that you can't push them to open up if they don't want to.

'Good. I'm glad you like her. She's a diamond,' said William.

A light bulb flashed on in my head. 'That's it! Destiny. Diamond. Diamond destiny.'

'Pardon?'

I quickly filled him in on the fundraising events (or lack of them) at our school and how we were holding a dance in May and were looking for a name or theme for it. 'Don't you see,' I finished. 'The Diamond Destiny Dance. Everyone can come glammed up to the eyeballs.'

'Yeah. Sounds good . . . but in the meantime, what about us?

I'm away for the Easter holidays. Spain, it's been booked for ages but what about before that? I wondered if we could . . . you know? What do you think?'

'Ah . . . yes. Um. A definite maybe.'

'A definite maybe?'

'Yeah. But you have to pass my test sometime.'

William laughed again. 'You're kidding?'

'Nope.' I wasn't going to fall back into his arms just because he was such a great kisser or because his sister was ill. No. It was time to play hard to get. Or at least, a bit.

'So what is this test?' he asked.

'I'll e-mail it to you while you're away. Give me your e-mail address.'

'It's easy: w.lewis@fastmail.com.'

I jotted it down.

'And yours?' he asked.

'Nestahotbabe@retro.co.uk.'

'Cool,' he said.

'And in the meantime, what's your favourite cake?' I asked.

'*Cake?* What has cake got to do with anything? Is that the test? If I say the right cake you'll go out with me?'

'No. That's not the test. Just tell me your favourite cake.'

'Coffee and walnut.'

'Right. Thanks. I might bake you one.'

'You're a strange girl, Nesta Williams.'

'You ain't seen nothing yet, babe,' I said.

I could hear him laughing softly at the other end of the phone. It was going to be fun carrying out Eleanor's request.

'I've agreed to do your test when I get it,' he said. 'So will you agree to go out with me before we leave for Spain.'

'When are you leaving?'

'Saturday morning. So how about Friday evening?'

'Um.' Take it slow this time, said a voice in my head.

'OK,' said the voice that came out of my mouth.

An A–Z of Party Themes

A: African, Aztec, animals, *Alice in Wonderland*, Adam and Eve, Arabian Nights.

B: Beatniks, black and white, *Beauty and the Beast*, all in blue, beggars and knights, bad taste, blonde bombshells.

C: Cops and robbers, cowboys and Indians, Chinese, cartoon characters, come as you were (in a past life).

D: Devils and angels, doctors and nurses, Dickens characters, diamonds (wear all your bling).

E: Egyptian, Elizabethan, Edwardian.

F: Fairies and goblins, fat, *The Flintstones*, flowers or fruit, fave fictional character

G: Gods and goddesses, gangsters and molls, glamour, ghosts, gender swap (boys as girls and girls as boys), Goth, *Grease* (come as a character from the movie) or Greece (dressed in the national dress).

H: Hollywood (dress for the Oscars), Hawaiian, horror, hats, heroes and heroines, Harry Potter, hippies.

I: Idols, Indian.

J: Japanese.

K: Knights and damsels in distress.

L: Legends, lords and ladies

M: Marx brothers, Mexican, monsters, masks, milkmaids and farmers.

N: Nuns and priests

O: Oriental, orange

P: Pyjamas, all in purple, police men and women, Pre-Raphaelite, punk.

Q: Queens and kings.

R: Rock stars, Fifties rock and roll, all in red, Renaissance, Romans and Britons.

S: Sci-fi, *Star Trek*, all in silver, school uniforms, Shakespearean characters, superheroes.

T: Thunderbirds, toga, Twenties, teddy boys and girls, toddlers and teddies, toys.

U: Uniforms.

V: Vicars and tarts, Victorian.

W: Walt Disney characters, whore or holy, all in white, witches and warlocks.

Z: Zzzzzzz . . . attend in your night wear.

If you don't have a lot of money to spend on costumes, the simpler the theme, the easier it is, e.g. all in blue, pyjamas, gender swap or everyone wearing a hat.

Try and find a music track appropriate for the theme, e.g. Egyptian music if going for an Egyptian theme, music from the 1920s if going for the Roaring Twenties theme.

Chapter 10

Do-Good
Disasters

Miss Watkins loved our fundraising suggestions. She gave us the go-ahead for just about everything but the sponsored sky diving and plans went straight into top gear.

'I knew you girls would breathe some fresh air into it all,' she said with a smile after we'd read our list out in the afternoon break. 'Now. No time to lose. Nesta, you can start by making an appeal for volunteers tomorrow and the rest of you, organise who's doing what and when and report back to me regularly. We have five weeks, three of which are in the Easter holidays so let's see if we can get some things organised to happen then.'

At assembly the next morning, I felt nervous when Mrs Allen, our headmistress, introduced me after she had made the usual announcements. Usually I don't mind performing in public, like if I'm in a play or something because then I'm not being me. I'm in disguise as some character. But this time I was going to speak as Nesta Williams and part of me was dreading it. I looked out at the sea of faces and took a deep breath.

'Good morning, everyone,' I started.

'Good morning,' everyone said back and I almost got the giggles as they all looked so serious. I had to resist the urge to do something stupid like tap dance or do my gangster rapper impersonation.

I took another breath, told myself to get it together, then continued. 'Imagine one of your family was dying or ill or homeless or lonely,' I read from the speech I had prepared last night. 'How would you feel? Yeah. Rotten. Most of us don't even think about such things. It's not happening to us so who cares? We're OK. Most of our families are OK. We have homes. We have food to eat, clothes to wear. Our health is good. But loads of people on the planet don't have our advantages.

'All I'm asking for is a bit of your time. Maybe an hour or two a week for the next few weeks in the holidays and you can make a difference. We're aiming to raise fifty thousand pounds to donate to a local hospice. It's a place where terminally ill teenagers go to spend their last weeks and the aim of the people who run the hospice is to make the place as much like home for them as possible. We're the lucky ones. Hopefully we all have years ahead of us to pursue careers, to travel, to fall in love, er . . . particularly to fall in love. The people who end up in hospices like the one we want to help won't have those chances. Please don't turn away this chance to do something . . .'

I was about to wind up as Mum had advised me that the

most important rule of public speaking is KISS (keep it short, stupid) but when I looked out at the sea of faces in the hall looking back at me, I wanted to be sure that they understood what I was saying.

'Just look around you,' I continued. 'Who knows where illness is going to strike. It could be one of the people standing in the hall with us today. It could be you. It *is* someone I met recently and only last year, she was standing in assembly like we are today and she was healthy and happy with a great future. Now she knows she hasn't got long to live. The people who run the hospice want to make those last weeks as comfortable as possible. A place where their friends and family can be with them. That's all anyone can do.

'I'm not going to go on and on at you as I think those of you who want to hear and do something don't need it repeated. We've got some fab activities planned to make money over the Easter holidays. We need volunteers for everything from selling raffle tickets to walking dogs. So, if you want to be involved, don't walk away, sign up at the back after assembly. And anyone who wants to buy tickets for the Diamond Destiny Dance on May 7th, then please get them from the back. It's going to be the event of the decade. Please help. Make your destiny a diamond one. Um. Yeah. Rock on.'

The response was phenomenal and we got loads of people signing up from all years and even Doreen and her pals looked pleased with the way things were going.

We didn't have long to get everything sorted before we broke up so Izzie, TJ, Lucy and I spent every spare moment getting contact details from volunteers, so that we could give them all something to do in the holidays. It wasn't too difficult to co-ordinate a timetable of events, allocate people to each one and we were off fundraising. Even Tony and Lucy's brothers, Lal and Steve, and their mates wanted to be involved in some way.

'This is going to be the best time ever,' I said as I walked out of school with TJ on the last day of term. At last it was the Easter holidays and I had a date with William in a couple of hours' time. It felt good to know that I'd be able to tell him that we were going to do something positive to help. I was confident that we'd reach the target and more.

I got home and went to have a bath before changing into my seduction outfit for the evening. I'd arranged to meet William in Crouch End and go for a cappuccino and then a walk. His mum wanted him back at a reasonable hour because they were taking an early morning flight. I heard the phone go when I was in the bath but thought nothing of it.

A few moments later, Mum knocked on the door. 'Nesta,' she said. 'That was William Lewis. He said he's sorry but he can't make it tonight.'

I was about to get out of the bath. 'Does he want to speak to me?'

'No, love,' said Mum. 'He's gone. I asked if he wanted a word with you and he asked if I'd pass the message on.'

'Does he want me to call him?'

Mum was quiet. I got the answer without her having to say anything. I lay back in the bath and submerged my head in the water. I sooooo wished I hadn't agreed to go out with him.

When I got out of the bath, I went to see if he'd tried to e-mail me. But nothing. I felt cold inside. Dumped before we'd even had a date. Well stuff you, William Lewis, I thought. I'm not going to even let this minor blip affect me in the slightest. I am going to throw myself into all the fundraising activities we have planned and not give you another thought. We're going to raise a million and when you come back from Spain, you can forget any chance you thought you were in with. This girl is moving on.

My first job was going to be a breeze. Mum had told all the neighbours about the fundraising scheme and one of them, Mrs Matthews, had asked if I'd check in on her house while she was away visiting her daughter for a couple of days. Easy peasy money. Twenty quid to look after her budgies and water a few plants.

'Now you make sure you talk to Charlie in particular,' said Mrs Matthews after she'd gone over the instructions for the fiftieth time. 'He's the one at the back, see?' She pointed to a bright blue budgie at the back of the cage.

'Oh, I will,' I assured her.

Mrs Matthews' eyes filled with tears. 'He's special, is Charlie. He was a gift from my late husband and – you make sure you look after him well. He likes it if you talk to him.'

No problem, I thought as I waved her off. Bit of water, bit of bird seed, bit of a chat. What could possibly go wrong?

All went well on the Saturday and Sunday and then Lucy and I turned up on Monday afternoon to find that Charlie was lying at the bottom of his cage with his little legs in the air.

'Ohmigod,' I said when I saw him.

Lucy gave the bird a gentle poke. It didn't move. 'This parrot is dead,' she declared.

'It's not a parrot. It's a budgie.'

'Whatever. It's dead.'

'Nooooooo, it can't be,' I cried. 'What am I going to do?'

'It wasn't your fault,' said Lucy. 'You did everything you were asked.'

'Should I try mouth to mouth?' I asked. 'Take it to the vets?'

Lucy shook her head. 'It's dead, Nesta. Not breathing. Look, just explain what happened. There was nothing you could do. It was just Charlie's time, that's all.'

'Maybe but I know she'll blame me. She's bound to. And Charlie is her favourite. Oh God.' I felt completely freaked out as I imagined Mrs Matthews coming back and finding her dead bird.

'Look,' said Lucy, 'we have to stay calm. Don't panic. Here's what we do. We'll buy another one. I bet I know exactly where they got it from as there's only one place that sells them round here. The pet shop in Muswell Hill. Mum gets squirrel nuts for Lal in there.'

'Squirrel nuts for Lal? Now I know your family is mad.'

'No. *He* doesn't eat them. He likes to feed the squirrels in the garden. You know what he's like about animals. He feeds the fox, the squirrels, the birds. It's a regular wildlife park in our back garden. So come on . . . let's go. Last time I was in the shop, they had a whole wall of birds. What time will Mrs Matthews be back?'

I checked my watch. 'Nine this evening.'

'And it's almost five now,' said Lucy. 'We just have time.'

We raced down to the pet shop as fast as we could. The shop keeper was just locking up and shook his head when I knocked on the door.

'Please,' I mouthed through the door but he just carried on locking up. I got down on my knees on the pavement and prayed to him and this time, he did take notice. He laughed and opened the door.

'All right then. So what is it you need so desperately?'

'A budgie.'

'And that can't wait until morning?'

I shook my head. 'Absolutely one hundred percent urgent.'

The shop keeper sighed. 'Always the same with you kids. Want it now and then three weeks later, you've lost interest.'

'No. No, I promise,' I said. 'It's not like that.'

The shop keeper relented. 'Come on in then. They're round the back. Let me know which one you want and be quick about it.'

Lucy and I ran through and quickly scanned the cages.

There were cages of finches and budgies all tweeting sweetly away.

'Perfect,' cried Lucy as she spied the last cage. In there was a budgie the exact same colour as Charlie. It was so perfect in fact, it looked like his twin.

'How much are they?' I asked.

'Twenty quid,' said the shopkeeper. 'Made your minds up have you?'

We nodded and soon were paying for the bird and hotfooting it back to Mrs Matthews where we replaced the dead bird with the live one. Lucy wrapped the real Charlie up in tissue and took him away with her to give him a proper burial in their back garden.

For the next couple of days, I was on tenterhooks waiting for Mrs Matthews' to notice the difference and call to complain, but she didn't. It was on the Friday night that she called me over when she saw me passing her house.

'Er, how's Charlie?' I asked as casually as I could.

'Extraordinary,' said Mrs Matthews, smiling. 'All this time I thought Charlie was a boy but I must have been wrong?'

'Oh. Why's that?' I asked.

'He laid an egg yesterday,' she said. 'I think my Charlie is a Charlotte.'

For a moment, I thought she might have rumbled me but no, she seemed to genuinely think that she'd mistaken Charlie's sex when he was first given to her. Ah well, I thought. Although I hadn't made a penny at least I still had a happy customer.

Lal and his mates were confident that they would make some fast money by offering to hand wash cars and set off on the Saturday in the sunshine with buckets and cloths in hand. In the meantime, TJ and I set off to do a stint of dog walking. Six dogs that belonged to various neighbours – I took three, TJ took three. At five quid for each dog, I thought, it should be no problem and we'd make our first bit of profit.

At twelve o'clock, Lal called us to say that they still hadn't got one job.

'We're in Shakespeare Gardens and have checked the whole area. Cleanest cars in the country,' he said. 'This calls for new tactics.'

TJ and I were doing the circuit at Cherry Tree Woods and were barely keeping up with the dogs who insisted on dragging us along for all they were worth. 'Tactics? And they are?' I asked as I pulled on the leads.

'We're going to dirty the cars up,' said Lal. 'Then they'll have to employ us.'

'*No*, Lal. That's a *mad* idea. No, please don't . . .' I pleaded into the phone but it was no use, he'd hung up.

'What's up?' asked TJ when she saw my face.

'We have to find the boys,' I said. 'Lal and his mates can't get any customers for the car wash. They're going to try dirtying them up.'

'Oh *nooooooo*,' cried TJ. 'We have to stop them. Really bad idea. There's been a spate of kids vandalising cars round where they've gone. I read about it in the local rag. People might think it's Lal and his mates. Do you know exactly what road he's on?'

I nodded. 'Shakespeare Gardens.'

I tried calling Lal's phone but the little rat wasn't answering. We both looked at the dogs who were almost chewing off their leads in their eagerness to finish their walk.

'You go. I'll stay here with the dogs,' she said.

'You sure you can handle six?'

She looked at the dogs and nodded. 'Just get back here fast.'

I legged it as fast as I could out of the park, up the alleyway and ten minutes later, I spotted the boys running down Springcroft Avenue. They were being chased by a very irate bald man. I quickly ducked down into the nearest garden and hid behind a rhododendron bush. It looked like they could outrun the man and I didn't want him to spot me and think I was with them. Unluckily, the owner of the house whose garden I was in saw me through her front window. A moment later, she had opened her door and was coming at me with a broom.

'Out, out,' she said. 'I'll have the police on you.'

'No. I'm sorry. I was – I'm not dangerous. I'm not a burglar or a vandal anything!'

'That's what they all say,' she said as she brandished her broom in my face. 'Get out of my garden.'

I decided to give up on the boys and ran back to Cherry Tree Woods. Poor TJ was almost having a heart attack by the time I got back there. She'd tied five of the dogs to a park bench from where they were all barking their objections at being kept on their leads and doing their best to drag the bench along behind them. TJ was chasing after Bonzo, a border collie, who had escaped his lead. He was causing havoc running after all the other dogs and their owners like it was a game. The dog walkers weren't at all pleased at their dogs being harassed and one of them told us in no uncertain terms to control our animal.

We tried everything but no matter what we did, he wouldn't come back. We called him. I tried throwing sticks and he ran for them but wouldn't bring them back.

'I know what will work,' said TJ after what felt like an

eternity of us running around like lunatics. 'Food. Go and buy a hamburger or hot dog, anything with meat in it and he'll soon come back.'

I raced to the nearest café on the High Street, back to the park and sure enough, it worked a treat. Bonzo was soon back on his lead. The others however were howling louder than ever having seen that one of their group got food and they didn't.

TJ looked at me and I nodded. Back I went to the café, returning with a big bag of burgers. The dogs wolfed them gratefully in seconds but at least they were quiet after that.

'Remember what I said about dog walking being a great way of meeting boys? A good pulling tactic?' I asked.

TJ laughed. 'Only people that got pulled were us. In every direction by the dogs!'

We returned the dogs to their owners but once again, our profit had been eaten into. Literally.

In the evening after the dog walking disaster, I turned on my computer and checked my e-mails for the first time that week. There was one from William, sent from an Internet café a couple of days ago.

Dear Nesta,
I am so sorry for last Friday. It's been a hellish time. Eleanor's consultant wanted to check her over before we flew to Spain which is why I couldn't make our date as she wanted me to go with her. He wasn't too happy about the results of her

blood tests and she really freaked as she'd been looking forward to this trip for months. Dad insisted that Olivia and I went out to Spain as planned and Mum stayed with Eleanor who was allowed to join us on Monday. It's been a roller coaster since then. She seemed fine when she arrived and then went under and at first we thought we'd have to fly her back and well, I don't want to go on. She's OK now but as I said, it's an up and down ride. It makes her so unhappy when she can't do the things that she had planned. Anyway, that was the reason I couldn't make it on Friday. Sorry and I hope to meet up sometime when I'm back. I haven't got my computer out here and am using an Internet café but you could text me back if you're still speaking to me. William.

I read the e-mail about ten times. That will teach me, I thought. I'd totally assumed that he'd let me down for all the wrong reasons. Assume. Dad always says: the first three letters of the word assume are ass. And I'd been an almighty one. I texted him back.

STL SPEKNG 2 U. DOING TONS OF FUNDRAYSG. GOING GUD. GONNA RAISE ££££££££££ 4 HOSPICE.

I hoped that would cheer him up.

And in the meantime, there were all those £££££ to raise. Izzie and her friend Ben (from the band she sings with) signed up to do gardening in the second week but they only lasted an hour as Ben had got a bit over enthusiastic with the shears and cut back someone's prize rose thinking that it was dead. Both of them were banned from the area and the man whose garden it was threatened to let all the neighbours know if Ben didn't pay for a replacement. Cost a fortune as it was a rare type of rose.

Once again, out went any profits.

For a while it looked as though Lucy was on a winner in the first week as she managed to get a load of people to donate bottles of spirits and she talked others (including Izzie) into giving away their Easter eggs. Whisky, vodka, gin, brandy and chocolate. She sold a load of raffle tickets and at last, it seemed that we might be in profit. Sadly, she had stored the bottles of donated spirits at her house and Lal and his mates decided to try them all out and replace what they drank with water. A trick that he'd managed to get away with before but when the raffle was drawn and the bottles were given away as prizes, the winners complained. They could tell that the bottles had been watered down and demanded compensation. Lucy tried pleading that it was for charity but was told in no uncertain terms that in that case she should be more professional about it. Lucy got her dad to replace the watered down bottles with the real stuff which meant that once again, the profit kitty was emptied but this time not for long. Lucy's mum found out what the boys had done and insisted that they pay up for what they had done out of their pocket money.

And the Easter eggs? The daft muffin left them in a bag by a radiator and they all melted. (Lucy daren't tell Izzie.)

In other parts of North London, other activities were taking place, and Mrs Owen was delighted with that fact that we'd managed to set up a rota of volunteers to help at the charity shop at weekends for the rest of the year.

Sadly, the candle-making sessions, led by Izzie, were a complete and utter disaster as the end results looked more like misshapen potatoes than candles. And her team had invested their pocket money to buy everything needed like wax and moulds and when they didn't sell, Izzie had to fork out to replenish their funds.

Candice Carter had volunteered to organise a sponsored fast and reported back to us that it was very popular. Apparently about twenty girls signed up for it but Candice finally admitted that most of them didn't actually have sponsors. They thought that it was an ace way to lose weight quickly. One of the girls fainted one lunchtime and confessed all to her mum who let the other parents know what was going on and they put a stop to it. So that was the end of that. Profit nil.

The swim-a-thon on the last Saturday of the holidays was going great, until Steve got cramp and had to be rescued by the life guard. And I got my period and got a different kind of cramp. Poor Steve could hardly walk when he got out the baths so called a cab to take him home and he dropped me off on the way. He paid for the cab with the small amount of sponsorship money he'd raised and offered to pay it back but it was only a couple of pounds.

'Hardly going to make much difference,' said TJ sadly as she did the accounts. 'But we've still got almost two weeks . . .'

TJ, Izzie and I nodded back at her and tried to look hopeful but I knew that inside they were feeling like I did. Desperate.

Things didn't improve.

Last on our list of fundraising activities to try was face painting and we held a session for kids in the car park outside the local supermarket. Once again, it was a fine clear day for April and a couple of girls from Year Eleven at school, Izzie and I set ourselves up and charged a pound for each face that we painted. It was going great with happy toddlers running about looking like bunnies and lions and clowns. And then one little girl had an allergic reaction to the paint and her face swelled up. Although we cleaned her up as fast as we could and it looked like no lasting damage had been done, her mother went crazy and threatened to sue the school. We did the grown-up, responsible thing and packed up our stuff and ran for it.

At least one idea was a success. TJ and Lucy had got the local nursery to donate some fabulous plants to sell at the jumble sale on the last Sunday of the holidays and they sold out before lunchtime. Phew.

Also at the jumble sale, we raised a small sum of money by asking people to guess how many coins there were in a jar. It was all going well until an old lady guessed correctly and we had to hand the lot over to her. TJ tried to persuade her to donate her winnings to charity but she was having none of it and told TJ to get lost in a rather colourful manner.

Next was the 'guess Miss Watkins's age' competition. TJ took a Polaroid of her and it was great fun going round the hall with sheets of paper where people could put down their guesses. No one got it right and most had added on about ten years to her real age. We were in profit at the end of the competition but Miss Watkins was well miffed at the age that people estimated her as and said she's going to go on one of those make-over programmes where they lift everything!

At the end of the sale, we added up everything that had come in over the past weeks from all the various activities. It came to just under a thousand pounds. I couldn't believe it.

'I thought we'd make so much more.' I sighed as I looked at the figures. 'After three weeks of pretty much solid fundraising, we have ended up with enough to buy the hospice a few plants, but forget the new wing.'

'And I even donated my Easter eggs,' said Izzie.

Lucy looked at the floor sheepishly. 'Yeah, there were so many things going on,' she said as she scanned the accounts. 'But hey listen, there's almost a grand here. It's better than nothing.'

I nodded. But I was fast beginning to realise that the dopey Doreen's were right. Raising serious amounts money wasn't that easy after all.

Good ideas for raising money for charity:

Sponsored walks/runs/swim-a-thons.

Raffle tickets for a good prize

(make sure the prize is donated so that you don't have to fork out for it from your profits).

Auction any of the better items donated in jumble.

Home services: cleaning, gardening, taking care of pets while people are away, car washing, carrying groceries.

Plant sale arranged with local nursery.

Games or quiz night.

Candle-making.

Charity ball.

Guess the age of your teacher.

Guess the number of coins in a jar.

Calendar sale.

Sport's tournament (good chance to get boys involved).

Recipe books – including teachers faves etc.

Spelling competition.

Shootout (football goals).

Book sale.

Cake sale.

Kiss-o-gram.

Invite a guest speaker to the school and sell tickets.

Face painting (be careful to use hypo-allergenic products).

Art sale. Best of some Year's work.

Star

'The good news is that King Noz have agreed to play for free at the DDD, Diamond Destiny Dance,' Izzie announced as we sat round the table at her house after the jumble sale to go over plans for the next couple of weeks.

'The bad news is that we're back to school tomorrow and we still have forty nine thousand pounds to raise,' I said. 'And still only a third of the tickets sold.'

'Do the dopey Doreens know about our slow start?' asked Lucy.

'Nope. And nor does Miss Watkins. I told her it was all going brilliantly. And if anyone tells them otherwise, I will have to kill them,' I replied. 'I couldn't bear to hear them saying, I told you so. No. Come on! We've got almost two weeks left. We will raise the money. We will.'

'Right,' said Izzie.

'Right,' said Lucy.

'Right,' said TJ.

Not one of them looked like they meant it. And if I was really honest I was beginning to have doubts myself. But I couldn't let that happen. It would mean letting Eleanor down. It would mean letting the hospice down. And it would mean letting William down. We'd been texting regularly since his e-mail from the Internet café and he seemed genuinely touched that we were bothering to try and raise the money. He'd also asked when I was going to put him through his 'test'.

Lucy must have picked up on my thoughts as she looked over at me and asked: 'Heard anything from your lover boy lately?'

'Yeah. He texts me every other day or so. I think we're becoming mates.'

'Only mates?' asked Izzie. 'Are you still being cautious because he's Luke's friend and you don't know if you can trust him?'

I shook my head. 'No. I think he's on the level, not like Luke at all so the fact that they know each other isn't a problem . . .'

'Then why just mates?' asked Izzie. 'I mean is that all you want after that snog at the jumble sale? To be *mates*?'

TJ laughed. 'Ah, but there are mates and mates aren't there? I mean there are mates like, say, Lucy and Tony . . .'

Lucy blushed. 'Well, we are.'

'Mates who snog a lot,' said Izzie.

'Yeah,' said TJ. 'And there are mates who you just hang out and have a laugh but wouldn't dream of locking lips with. So what kind are you and William going to be?'

'Um . . . not sure,' I said. I wasn't sure. After our first kiss, I knew that I wanted to be a lot more than mates but didn't know if he felt the same. It had been great texting him while he'd been away but I knew that he'd got back yesterday and part of me had hoped that he'd get in touch straight away and maybe even come over but I hadn't heard anything. I'd purposely not texted or called him so that he wouldn't think that I had been counting the days until his return. Even though I had. And I was beginning to realise that anything might have happened with Eleanor. She might have taken a turn for the worse.

Or maybe William was simply feeling low and not in the mood for talking. People often are when they come back from holidays and have to get back into their routines. Maybe he was feeling down because Spain might have been Eleanor's last holiday. I had no idea what was going on in his head. Maybe he wasn't that interested in me and the snog at the jumble sale had just been a one-off. 'I did say to him that I'd e-mail him a questionnaire . . .'

Izzie laughed. 'Questionnaire? Like you fill in when you want a job?'

'Yeah. To see if he is worthy of my attention.'

'Cool,' said Lucy.

'Anyway, with all the activities lately, I haven't had time to work it out, so I need you guys to help me.'

'Find out what star sign he is,' said Izzie. 'Put that as question number one then we can find out if you're compatible or not. Some star signs are much flirtier than others.'

'Like which?' asked TJ.

'Libras are the biggest flirts. Gemini's not far behind,' replied

Izzie. 'And Leo's are pretty bad too.'

'Nothing wrong with being a flirt,' I said as I wrote down Izzie's question as number one.

'I'd ask him what his idea of a perfect first date is,' said TJ. 'I think you can tell a lot about a boy by how he treats you the first time he takes you out.'

'True,' I said and wrote that down as number two.

At the end of the hour, we had ten good questions which Izzie typed into her computer.

'Have you got his e-mail address?' she asked.

I nodded. I knew it off by heart. 'w.lewis@fastmail.com.'

She typed it in.

'Oh God,' I said as we heard the ping that told us that the e-mail had gone. 'No going back now. I hope he doesn't take it the wrong way or anything. Or think I'm being too serious about it.'

'Doubt it,' said Izzie. 'Anyway, I think all boys we meet from now on should be asked those questions before any of us go out with them.'

'And it's too late to worry now,' said Lucy.

'What if he replies?' asked Izzie. 'Are you going to go on a date with him?'

'Yes. Sure. Eleanor asked me to cheer him up.'

'Yeah but what about you?' asked Lucy. 'How do you feel about him?'

'I haven't seen him for weeks,' I said. 'So. . . I don't know. I'll see how I feel when he gets in touch.'

That's *if* he gets in touch, I thought.

★ ★ ★

We went over the plans for the following week again and it was obvious that even if everything went without any more disasters, the likelihood of us raising all the money that was needed was pretty well impossible. For William or not, I thought, I do want this to work.

'It's not too late,' I said. 'What we need is something brilliant to bring in the crowds. So let's think. We've got King Noz for the show?'

Izzie nodded. 'And a good disco. A mate of Ben's, DJ Diggie said he'd do it for nothing.'

'Cool,' said Lucy. 'He's supposed to be really good. Some people will pay the price of the ticket just to see him.'

An idea began to form in my head. 'I know. I know what we need. Not so much a dance as an event. Not so much an event as a show . . .'

'Meaning?' asked TJ.

'What Lucy said. People will come to see DJ Diggie. So let's give them some *more* things to come and see.'

'Like what?' asked Izzie.

I had a sudden flash of inspiration. 'I know! What about combining the dance with a fashion show?'

Lucy nodded. 'Go on . . .'

'You could make up some new designs, Lucy,' I said. 'Plus, we could use some of the ones you've already made.'

'And we could ask DJ Diggie to put some sounds to a catwalk show,' I said.

'Yeah,' said TJ. 'We could ask some of the local clothes shops if they'd like to contribute. It could be good advertising for them.'

'But we need something else,' I said. 'Something to really draw in the crowds.'

'Such as?' asked Izzie.

'Such as — a supermodel,' I said.

'Yeah, right,' said Izzie. 'Like a supermodel is going to come to some backwater dance to model clothes — no offence, Lucy — made by a schoolgirl when she could be modelling Chanel? Get real, Nesta. These girls are used to modelling Gucci, Armani, Prada. They model in Milan, Paris, New York. Didn't one of them say she didn't get out of bed for less than ten thousand pounds? So why would one of them want to come to a hall in East Finchley?'

'Because we are going to ask them,' I said.

'But who? How?' asked TJ.

'Lucy. What was the name of that model you read about in *Vogue*?' I asked. 'The one who does charity work?'

'Star. Star Axford,' said Lucy.

'And didn't you say that she lives in London?' I asked.

'Yeah. Notting Hill, the article said.'

'I am going to find her and beg her to come to our dance and what's more, I'm going to ask her to model some of Lucy's clothes. She's bound to say yes — she sounded so nice from the article you read about her, Luce. How could she refuse such a good cause?'

'Excellent idea,' said Izzie.

'Worth a try but how do we find her?' asked TJ.

'How do you find anyone?' I said. 'Um. I'll ask my dad.'

Questionnaire for Boys

1) What is your star sign?
2) What is your idea of a perfect date?
3) Your girlfriend is out of town for a weekend and the school hot babe makes a play for you. Do you:
   a) Let her seduce you. What your girlfriend doesn't know won't hurt her?
   b) Reject her advances. You would never be unfaithful to your girlfriend?
4) Your best friend is a love rat and cheats on his girlfriends do you:
   a) Stay out of it and mind your own business?
   b) Tell the girls what is going on?
5) How many girlfriends have you had?
6) Are you still a virgin?
7) Describe your ideal woman?
8) What turns you off a girl?
9) What's your favourite chat-up line?
10) What is the best way to break up with someone?
   a) By text?
   b) Get your friend to do it for you?
   c) By phone?
   d) In person?

Chapter 12

Blagging
it

'Models Five,' said a lady's voice. 'How can I help you?'

Dad had been brilliant when I told him about my idea to get Star Axford on board. He'd made a couple of phone calls and soon came back to me with the number of Star's model agency.

'I . . . Hello. I . . . I need to get in touch with Star Axford,' I said as I gave the girls the thumbs up on Monday after school.

'Who may I say is calling?'

'Nesta Williams.'

'From where?'

'Er . . . From North London.'

'No, I mean from which company?'

'No company. It's a private call.'

'Are you a friend?'

'No.'

'Are you family?'

'No.'

'Can I ask what it's regarding?'

'I have to ask her something.'

'I'm afraid Miss Axford's agent isn't here at the moment but I can pass on any messages. Would you like to leave a message?'

'No, I mean yes, please,' I said, then I left my number.

That was Monday after school. I tried again on Tuesday and told the lady that it was urgent. She promised to pass the message on. Wednesday still no reply from them. And no reply from William.

'It's not going to happen this way,' I said to Tony as we had breakfast together on Thursday.

'Let me try,' he said.

'Like Star'd speak to you,' I said.

Tony raised an eyebrow at me. 'Just give me the phone and prepare to watch the Master.'

He went through the same routine. No result.

'Ha,' I said. 'Big Head. Not as easy as it seems is it?'

'Give me the phone again,' he said. 'Winners never quit and quitters never win. Only losers give up.'

Once again I passed him the portable, he dialled and my jaw dropped open in amazement as he went into an Oscar winning performance.

'*Ciao. Si.* Thees is Antonio Costello. I phoning from *Vogue* Milano. I needa to be in touch with a Star Axford,' he said in a thick Italian accent (which isn't too hard for him as Dad's Italian). '*Si. No.* No need leave message. We have shoot next week. I need to know, is she on location out of the country or is she there in England at the moment? I fly there next week. If she no available, I find someone else. No problem. *Si*. Thank you. Oh? She at Olympia? Today? Oh *si*, *si*. Of course. I knew. I forget. And she there next week? Thank you, thank you. I ring you back immediately.' He put the phone down and grinned. 'She's doing a show at Olympia.'

'Wow. You really are the Master,' I said. I was impressed. I think even I would have been taken in by his act.

'So get on the Net. Look up what the show is at Olympia and get the details. Find the times and get down there,' said Tony.

A quick look on the Olympia website told us that there was a three day show on this week. Today was the first day and there were two shows: one at two o'clock and another at four. There was no way I could make the early one because of school but I might make the end of the four o'clock one if I left as soon as we got out.

As soon as the girls heard that I was off to Olympia, they insisted on accompanying me. Sadly, it seemed that everything was conspiring against us. Mr Johnson was still giving out our English assignment way after the bell at the end of class so in the end, Izzie stuck her hand up and said, 'Look sir, normally we don't mind staying behind but we have urgent work to do this evening.'

Mr Johnson looked at her wearily. 'Oh, something you don't want to miss on the telly, Miss Foster?'

'No, sir. We have charity work to do,' said Izzie in as important voice as she could muster. 'We have to go and enlist the services of a celebrity guest.'

Mr Johnson didn't look as if he believed a word of it but he relented. 'Oh very well, then. Go on. I've had enough of you all for one day anyway.'

Izzie, Lucy, TJ and I got up and ran for it. Raced to the bus, raced to the Tube and all was going well until it decided to stop at Camden.

'All change,' said a voice over the tannoy. 'This train will terminate here.'

'Oh no,' I said. 'We're never going to make it and the four o'clock is the last show.'

We got off the Tube and it seemed an eternity before the empty one moved off and another one arrived and at last we were on our way again. A quick change at Embankment onto the District line, *another* change at Earl's Court and at last we were at Olympia.

We ran to the entrance where a security guard asked to see our tickets.

'Tickets? Oh God,' I said. 'I didn't think. Tickets.' I'd been so focused on getting there, I hadn't thought about getting in. 'How much are they?'

'Fifteen pounds each but that was for the whole event. You've missed most of today. Not worth it for the last ten minutes,' said the guard.

We each found our purses and looked to see how much money we had between us. I had a fiver, Izzie had three pounds, Lucy one pound fifty and TJ only fifty pence. Not even enough to get one of us in.

'We could always do a Florence,' said Lucy with a grin,

referring to the time when we were on our school trip in Italy and we got stranded with no money so we tried busking.

'No way and no time,' I said as I racked my brain for what to do next. It felt so frustrating that Star was only a stone's throw away and yet I couldn't get near her.

'No, don't do a Florence,' said Izzie. 'Do a Tony.'

I'd told the girls how Tony had got the information from the model agency this morning and like me, they had been well impressed.

'Yeah,' said Lucy. 'If he could blag his way into finding out where Star was by pretending to be a photographer, you could blag your way in by pretending to be a model.'

'Yeah,' said TJ. 'People are always saying that you could be one if you wanted to be. Go for it.'

'Yeah but . . .'

'Come on, Nesta,' said Izzie. 'Now's the time to find out if what people said was for real.'

'I ca—' I was about to say I can't but in the same breathe, I decided I could. What had I to lose? But I had to act quickly before I lost my nerve. I pulled the girls away from the steps and round a corner out of sight of the main entrance and security people.

'I need to tart up a bit,' I said. 'Lucy. Lip-gloss.'

Lucy handed me some lip-gloss which I quickly applied.

'Izzie, hair brush.'

Izzie quickly brushed my hair.

'TJ, eye make-up.'

'Haven't got any.'

'Don't worry, I have some,' said Lucy handing me a wand of mascara and a stick of soft grey liner to smudge around my eyes.

Two minutes later, I was ready but as I went to go back round the corner, I felt my stomach turn over with nerves. 'Oh God, I can't do it,' I said.

'Why not?' asked Lucy.

'I'm shy.'

'Too bad,' said Izzie. 'This is important!'

'Yeah, we've come this far,' said Lucy. 'You can do it. I know you can.'

'Pretend that you're a character in a movie,' said Izzie. 'That usually helps you be brave.'

'Right,' I said. 'Who?'

'Er . . .' Izzie replied. 'Er . . . Um. Braveheart? James Bond?'

'They're men!' I said.

'OK. Uma Thurman in *Kill Bill*,' said Lucy. 'I haven't seen it but my brothers said she was a spectacular heroine.'

'I *have* seen it,' I said. 'And it's probably not the best role model for this situation as she kills just about everyone who crosses her path. I'm going to try and find Star not kung fu the security guards and then wipe out the audience in a blood bath on my way to her.'

'*Climb every mountain*,' Lucy began to sing in a really awful warbly voice. '*Follow every stream . . .*'

'And I am *not* going to pretend that I am Julie Andrews in *The Sound of Music*,' I said. 'She was a nun not a potential model.'

'Julia Roberts in *Pretty Woman*,' said TJ.

Izzie looked at her watch. 'We're running out of time, guys . . .'

'OK. So think of *why* you're doing it,' urged TJ. 'Try and remember that and you might find that it helps overcome your shyness.'

I nodded. 'Yes. Course. I can do it. I will. Now you girls go and distract the guard we were talking to earlier while I try to get in.'

The girls did as they were told and soon had the guard's attention. I flew up the steps behind them as if I was in a terrible hurry.

A lady to the left of the main door waved me over to her. 'Where are you going, miss?' she asked.

I decided to do a Tony after all. '*Scusi,*' I said with an Italian accent. 'Excuse. I here for show. My train late. I so sorry. Which way for model's from Models Five? They going to keeel me.'

The lady didn't even blink. She opened the door for me and pointed down a corridor. 'Better hop it, love. It's down there but you'd better hurry. Show's almost over.'

'*Grazie, grazie,*' I said as I flew in and down in the direction she'd pointed.

Once inside I could hear loud throbbing music coming from behind wide doors. I quickly headed for the music and found myself inside a vast auditorium. Silver laser lights were swirling round the walls and it was hard to see properly in the dim light. My eyes soon grew accustomed to the dark and I could see the catwalk and stage spotlighted in the centre of the hall. It looked like a fun show as I got closer and stood behind the seating area. Models in silver and blue shiny outfits and enormous rubber platform boots danced and strutted down the aisle in time to a funky soundtrack that was pumping through ginormous speakers on either side of the stage. What a shame Lucy didn't get in as well, I thought, as she would have loved this.

I made my way as close as I could and stood watching at the back. In front of me, I could see the back of heads of rows and rows of people all intent on watching the show.

I bent down to ask a lady sitting in front of me. 'How much longer?' I asked.

'Almost finished,' she whispered. 'Now shhhhhh.'

A couple more models bounced and bumped along the catwalk but there was no sign of Star. I hoped she hadn't been in the earlier show and then left. All of a sudden, all the lights went out. The hall was silent. And then out of the speakers blasted a funky version of the wedding march. Spotlights hit the stage and there she was. Star Axford.

She looked totally amazing in what looked like a wedding outfit for a character out of *Star Trek*. It was in ankle-length, figure-hugging, shiny silver silk fabric, with a train flowing out like a waterfall at the back. On her arms she was wearing long silver gloves. Round her head she was wearing a silver mesh veil and a space-age tiara, with what looked like three crescent moons and a star attached. Everyone cheered as she floated up and down in front of them. Moments later, a bald man with a pink goatee beard appeared and the crowd went mad again. All the models who had appeared earlier came out to join the man and Star and the cheers grew louder.

Now's the time to get backstage, I thought as I edged my way closer and closer to the stage. Luckily, everyone was so intent on watching the catwalk that no one noticed me slip behind the vast black curtain and into the models' dressing area.

'Who are you?' said an unfriendly voice behind me.

I turned to see a severe-looking lady all in black staring at me suspiciously. Blag it Nesta, blag it. It's all for a good cause.

'I Carla's seester,' I said getting back into my Italian persona. 'She out there. She say meet her back here.'

The woman looked me up and down with a bored expression and she must have decided that I didn't look like trouble, as she turned away and lit a cigarette.

After several encores, the models began to drift back into the dressing area. Bottles of champagnes started popping and glasses were filled. This is sooo glamorous, I thought, as I watched everyone, and for a moment, I was so caught up in it all that I almost forgot why I was there.

I quickly scanned the girls for a sign of Star and spotted her on the far side of the room. She was changing out of the wedding dress and into jeans and a T-shirt. I made my way over to her and watched for a second as she sat at a dressing table and began to wipe off her make-up. She really was pretty. A perfect pixie face with fabulous high cheek bones, beautiful silver blue eyes and short blond hair that was spiked up for the show. I could see exactly why the designer had picked her for his collection. She looked like an alien princess. I wondered what was the best moment to talk to her as I didn't want to disturb her routine. I waited until it looked as if she had almost finished, then I crept a bit closer.

'Er . . . Star . . .'

'Yes?' she replied as she turned round.

'I'm Nesta Williams. Can I have a quick word?'

Star looked around the room. 'Are you from a magazine?'

'No. Nothing like that. I came to ask you an enormous favour.'

For a moment Star's expression grew weary, but she didn't say anything.

'I . . . that is we . . . at our school we're doing a fundraising event for a hospice for the terminally ill. And I wondered . . .'

'Nesta, I think it's lovely. And I wish you every success but I don't carry my diary with me and you really need to talk to my agent as he deals with this kind of thing.'

'Oh, but it won't take a moment. Can you come to a dance a week on Saturday? We're doing a fashion show as well and . . .'

By this time, a security lady had noticed me and was making her way over. 'This girl bothering you, Star?' she asked.

Star shook her head. 'No. Not bothering exactly . . .'

'So will you come?' I asked.

Star stood up and picked up her bag from the dressing table. 'I have to go now Nesta and I'm sorry. I get at least a hundred requests like this every week. That's why I have to let my agent deal with them.' She slipped her hand into her bag and pulled out a card. 'Here's the number for his direct line. You can call him and see how the next few weeks are fixed but usually we book charity events months ahead.'

For a moment she hesitated, sighed and gently touched my arm. Then she was gone.

Winners never quit and quitters never win.

Chapter 13

Singing in the Rain

'There are other celebs,' said Lucy on the Tube home from Olympia.

'Yeah,' said Izzie. 'We don't need her. We have clothes, we have a venue, we have models to show the clothes.'

'And Mrs Owen said we can have a free rein in the charity shop on Saturday to look for anything for the show,' said TJ. 'She said she's already got a couple of bags of designer gear to give us.'

'And Lucy's been working late every night,' said Izzie. 'Haven't you Luce? She's got some hot little numbers ready to go.'

Lucy nodded. 'And Steve has been putting together a great soundtrack for the models to show the clothes to. He's been really enjoying it, I think. And he's offered to take photos on the night.'

I smiled weakly. I could see that they were doing their best to be positive but I knew that behind it all, they felt as disappointed as I did. 'But we still need to sell more tickets and we've only got one week left. I'd hoped Star coming would have boosted the sales.'

Lucy put her hand over one of mine. 'You tried, Nesta. That's all anyone can do.'

It was true. I had tried. I'd got my mobile out and phoned the number on the card that Star had given me as soon as I'd left the hall. A brisk sounding man answered and after I'd made my request, he had laughed and said that Star was booked up with events for the next year. 'Give us a bit of notice next time, love,' he said in a sarcastic tone before hanging up.

For the rest of the journey, we all sat in silence, lost in our thoughts. I kept thinking of what Tony had said this morning. Only losers give up.

'There must be a way,' I said to the girls when I reached my stop at Highgate and got up to get off the Tube.

'Yeah,' Izzie said, nodding. 'Speak later. We'll think of something.'

As I walked up the hill outside the station and made my way back to our flat, I passed a house where the occupants were doing some decorating. It was a funny sight because, through a window, I could see a father plastering paste onto wallpaper on a table and two of his kids were ready with the next piece from a roll to hand to him. They were struggling to keep the roll open and it kept curling back up, taking them with it.

When I got home, I went straight to my computer to see if William had responded to my questionnaire. My chest tightened when I saw that there was a message from him in the inbox. I was just about to open it when my mobile rang. It was Lucy.

'Star Axford's on TV,' she said. 'Channel Four news.'

I quickly flicked my set on and sure enough there was Star. The interviewer was asking her about her life as a supermodel.

'I suppose it's the high life and limos everywhere for you, is it?'

Star shook her head. 'Actually, no. I don't believe in waste when I have a perfectly good pair of legs. And here in London we have a great Tube system. I usually get the Tube to work and back. It's often far quicker than being stuck in traffic.'

'But don't you get recognised?'

Star laughed. 'I don't look like I do on the front covers when I've taken all the make-up off,' she said. 'So no, I don't often get recognised.'

Huh, I thought to myself. All that trouble to get into Olympia and I could have just waited by the Tube station for her!

I flicked off the telly and was about to go back to the computer when an idea flashed through my head. I quickly dialled Lucy.

'Did you see Star?' she asked.

'Yeah. I did. And I think we ought to go and try her again,' I said.

'Again? But why? Why do you think she would change her mind?'

'I'll tell you tomorrow my little munchkin. I have a plan that I think might just work.'

After I'd hung up, I went back to my computer, took a deep breath and opened William's e-mail.

There was no dear Nesta or anything. Just the questionnaire returned with his answers. Oh dear, I thought as I began to read his replies.

```
1) What is your star sign?
The Starbucks coffee sign. They do a mean coffee
and walnut muffin.


2) What is your idea of a perfect date?
23rd January 1893.


3) Your girlfriend is out of town for a weekend
   and the school hot babe makes a play for you.
   Do you:
     a) Let her seduce you. What your girlfriend
        doesn't know won't hurt her?
     b) Reject her advances. You would never be
        unfaithful to your girlfriend?
I haven't got a girlfriend at the moment. Can you
help?


4) Your best friend is a love rat and cheats on
   his girlfriends do you:
```

a) Stay out of it and mind your own business?

b) Tell the girls what is going on?

I haven't got a best friend. I have lots of friends. But no girlfriend. Can you help?

5) How many girlfriends have you had?

803, if you count my past life as a rabbit.

6) Are you still a virgin?

Not if you count my past life as a rabbit.

7) Describe your ideal woman?

My mum. Ahhh . . .

8) What turns you off a girl?

Girls with one eyebrow and three sets of nipples. Yuk.

9) What's your favourite chat-up line?

I have a questionnaire I'd like you to do before I'll go out with you. A very nice girl used this line on me recently.

10) What is the best way to break up with someone?

a) By text?

b) Get your friend to do it for you?

c) By phone?

d) In person?

By carrier pigeon.

His replies made me laugh out loud and all the doubts I'd had over the holidays melted away. He *was* interested in me. Part of me felt like phoning him and setting up a date right there and then but I remembered my resolve to listen to my own advice and take it slow this time.

Instead I e-mailed him:

`Mr Lewis. You did not take your test at all seriously. You will get detention. To be taken with Nesta Williams.`

He e-mailed back later that evening:

`Sorry I wasn't in touch before. Been back and forth to hospice with Eleanor. Long story but she's stable again. So when for my punishment? Soon I hope.`

I e-mailed back:

`L8R. Will be in touch. Probably weekend as first have a V. important mission.`

The next day, I got up early and went into school in time to catch Mrs Allen before school assembly. Luckily she was in her office and I asked if I could make another appeal for volunteers at assembly.

'Well, I have to admire your tenacity, Nesta,' she said after she'd heard me out. 'Why not? Give it a go.'

Ten minutes later, I was up on stage and once more looking out on that same sea of faces but this time I didn't have the giggles.

'Hi,' I said. 'Me again. Nesta, that is. As you know we're trying to raise funds for a hospice for the terminally ill, a place where their families can also stay so that the patients are not on their own all the time. It's not going great and I won't embarrass myself by telling you the paltry amount raised so far. But we still have another week to go until the dance – I hope you've already got your tickets. It's going to be a great night.

'The Diamond Destiny Dance will now also include a fashion show, and I've been trying to get a supermodel to come and join us. But first we need to get her to notice us. She told me that she gets a hundred requests a week like mine, so I thought, how about if she gets a request that she can't ignore? What I'm asking is that as many people as possible turn up at the Tube at Olympia tomorrow.

'The plan is that we line the area from the Tube to the hall. I'll be there with my mates with rolls of wallpaper and glue. All you have to bring is a letter asking if Star will come to the dance. Make the letters as bright as you can. Stick stars all over them. We'll stick the letter to the wallpaper and make a long roll of invites. That's all. Simple. And no one can say we didn't try. So that's it. Olympia Tube station. Four-thirty-ish tomorrow. Thank you and good night. I mean, good morning.'

'Nice one,' said TJ after I'd got down from the stage and made my way over to them. 'Good plan.'

'Absurd,' said Doreen coming up behind us. 'Invites on wallpaper. That's so tacky. No one will show. You wait and see.'

'I take it that you won't be coming then?' I asked.

Doreen gave me a look as if to say, 'Are you mad?'

I didn't care. It was worth a try.

On Saturday morning, Mum took me to Homebase and we bought rolls and rolls of plain wallpaper which Mum insisted on paying for as her contribution to the cause.

'That should be enough,' she said as we paid at the till. 'How many people are you expecting?'

'Um, eight so far,' I said. 'TJ, Lucy, Izzie and I. Tony said he'd come and so did Lucy's brothers, so that's Steve and Lal.'

'Lal?' asked Mum. 'Didn't you say that he was a liability?'

'He wants to make up for drinking all the booze,' I replied. 'Lucy said that she'd make sure he behaves. And Ben told Izzie that he'd come and he might bring a few guys from the band. It's a start.'

'I think it's marvellous what you're doing,' said Mum. 'Now let's get back because I have to get to work this afternoon.'

At three o'clock I met Izzie, TJ and Lucy at the Tube where they were waiting with Lal, Steve, Tony, Ben and Baz. Soon we were in place at Olympia ready to catch Star at the end of the show.

Izzie pulled her jacket tight round her, looked up at the sky and frowned. 'It's looking a bit like rain,' she said. 'I'm glad I brought my brolly.'

'No, no, it can't,' I said. 'Please, God. No rain.'

Ben began to do a mad Native American-type dance but

instead of going round in a circle, he danced backwards.

'What on earth are you doing?' asked Izzie.

'You've heard of the rain dance,' he replied. 'This is the no-rain dance.'

We'd all cracked up and did it with him and miracle of miracle, it did seem to dry up a bit. I like Ben. He's not my type – but he is cute with his stuck in the Sixties John Lennon look. It's a shame he and Izzie didn't work out because they are good together but then they've stayed friends which is more than I've managed to do with my ex-boyfriends. I might be friends with Simon if he wasn't up in Scotland but Luke, I haven't even seen him since before Christmas and he doesn't live far away. As we continued waiting outside Olympia, I wondered if William had said anything about us to him and how he'd feel if he knew that one of his friends was going to date one of his exes.

'Four o'clock,' said Lucy as she looked around the meeting place. 'Still no one here.'

'Four o'clock and one minute,' said TJ a minute later.

'Four o'clock and two minutes,' said Izzie a minute after that.

'Shut up, will you,' I said. 'For God's sake, chill. We said for people to meet here at four-thirty, there's loads of time yet.' But inside, I was worried that Doreen had been right and no one else was going to turn up and we'd be a small pathetic group holding our letters and our wallpaper up for no one to see.

'Come on,' said Lucy. 'Let's get organised, at least.' And she went into overdrive rolling out the wallpaper and sticking the sheets of paper with our individual invites onto it.

We had all written on different coloured paper so even though there weren't many letters yet, the display at least looked colourful – and Izzie had stuck bright blue stars all over hers. We held it up to see how long it was so far and it stretched out about four feet. I'd imagined that there would be hundreds of us, all holding up the wallpaper stretched out to fill the space between the Tube station and the entrance.

A Tube train rattled into the station and a number of people got off. I strained to see if there was anyone there from school but there only seemed to be a few commuters going the other way.

Another Tube, Still no one from school.

Another Tube. Still no one. And it was twenty past four.

Another Tube. And . . .

'Hey, there's Sara Jenkins and her mates from Year Nine,' said Lucy as she waved like a lunatic at them and they came to join us. A few minutes later, another group from Year Ten arrived. Then another lot. Then another. Then Candice Carter and all her mates. Before long most of our class had shown up. Lal looked as happy as a pig in muck when he realised how many girls were turning up and he quickly made himself useful pasting letters, unrolling more wallpaper and flirting for all he was worth. Steve took photos, as TJ said it would be a great shot for the school magazine and would show Doreen that she was wrong.

By four-forty, there was a fantastic crowd. We were all ready. We were all lined up, letters in place but where were the people from inside Olympia?

'Go and check,' I said to Tony. 'Maybe the show's running late today because it's the last night.'

Tony had just set off up towards the hall when the doors opened and crowds started flowing out.

'Ah, here they come,' I said. 'I reckon the models will follow in about ten or fifteen minutes. Keep your eyes peeled for Star everyone.'

The crowd coming out of Olympia were curious about the group of teenagers hanging about outside holding up an enormous roll of wallpaper and most of them stopped to either read the letters or ask what was going on.

'Can I take a photo?' asked an American man as he held up a camera.

'Go ahead,' I said, and after he'd taken his photo, he handed me twenty pounds.

'For your cause, ma'am,' he said. 'Good luck and have a nice evening.'

'Thank you,' I said.

And then a few others followed his lead and asked if they could make donations. Before long, I'd collected fifty pounds.

Slowly the crowd dispersed and the Tube carried most of them away. Only a few people were still drifting out of the hall.

'Do you know if Star Axford has left yet?' I asked one pretty young girl who looked like she might have been a model.

'Don't think so,' she said as she held her bag up over her head as it was beginning to drizzle.

'Oh God,' I said as I looked up at the sky then down the line of people. 'OK gang, everyone with a brolly stand next to someone without one and try and keep the paper dry.'

Luckily most of the girls from our school had brought umbrellas and up they went so that we could protect our wall of letters. Oh please come soon Star, I thought as the rain got heavier, please, or else there's only going to be a soggy mess for you to look at.

A few seconds later, a white van came whizzing round the corner, pulled up and a man and a woman got out. The man was carrying a camera and the other was a blonde lady I recognised as Monisha Harris. She worked as a roving reporter for the same cable station as Mum. I'd met her last summer when she came to our flat for one of the barbecues Mum likes to throw from time to time for her work colleagues. I nudged Izzie.

'Must have come to film the last show,' I said. 'Bit late.'

'They're coming over here,' said Izzie as the cameraman strode over in our direction.

'Where's Nesta Williams?' asked Monisha and someone pointed to me.

She walked over to me. 'Hi, Nesta. So what's all this about?' she asked as the man pointed the camera at me. 'Your mum sent us down here. Said there was a story for the early evening London news.'

Good old Mum, I thought. She must have mentioned that we were down here when she went in to do her shift.

'We're here to ask Star Axford to come to our school dance,' I said looking into the camera. 'It's in aid of the Lotus Hospice, North London, and we're trying to raise fifty thousand pounds so that they can build a new wing.'

Monisha asked me a few more questions and let me explain a little about the cause and then went down the line filming some of the letters.

It was then that Star came out.

'There she is,' said TJ pointing then waving. 'Star. *Star*. Over here.'

Star looked over at the line of people staring at her and waving and looked bemused. Monisha and the cameraman raced over to her and said something that I couldn't hear and then the skies really did open and the rain began to pour. The camera man held up his jacket for Star so that she didn't get wet and escorted her and Monisha back up the steps to the hall where they all disappeared.

'*Noooo*,' I cried. 'Hey Star, *Star*.'

We were all yelling. 'Star. STAR. *Staaaaaaaaarrrrr.*'

But she'd gone and we hadn't had a chance to show her our letters or make our request.

And by now it was pouring down.

'So much for your no-rain dance,' I said to Ben.

'Sorry,' he said with a shrug.

Everyone did the best that they could to stop the paper getting wet but the rain was coming down at an angle and it was hard to protect it. The ink began to run. The paper grew soft. Some of it disintegrated, turned to mush and tore. Soon all that was left was a coloured streak on the pavement and we were all getting wetter by the minute.

Tony looked at me, shrugged then began singing the song

from the movie, *Singing in the Rain* and dancing around like Gene Kelly. Ben joined in and then Steve and Lal who were soon followed by some of the girls. After a few minutes, loads of people were dancing, singing, getting soaked and having a great old time. Up on the steps of Olympia, I could see the cameraman laughing as he filmed it all.

I looked around at half our school splashing about in puddles with their hair plastered flat with rain.

'Well, that was a disaster,' I said as I let my umbrella go and joined in the mad rain dance.

Result

'Quick, quick, Tony, Nesta,' called Dad when we got home later that evening. 'You're on the local news.'

We raced into the living room to watch and there on the screen, in all our glory were about a hundred very wet teenagers singing and dancing outside Olympia. It looked like pandemonium but luckily the cameraman and Monisha Harris had grasped what we were trying to do.

'Ohmigod! It's me!' I gasped when suddenly I appeared on the screen explaining what it was all about.

After a few lines from me, it was cut to the line of paper before the sog set in with a voice-over from Monisha explaining why we were all there.

And then there she was with Star back inside Olympia.

'And so the big question is, Miss Axford, will you be accepting the invitation to this Diamond Destiny Dance?' asked Monisha.

I held my breath as I waited to hear Star's answer.

'I have a brother and sister about the age of everyone who

turned up this afternoon,' she said. 'I got to thinking, what if it was them out there asking me to go to their dance. So, Monisha, the answer is yes, I will be going.'

Tony and I threw cushions up into the air.

'Hurrah!' I cried. 'It worked.'

I raced to my room to get on the phone and make sure the others had seen it as well. And I couldn't resist calling William to tell him the good news.

'Yeah. I saw you,' he said. 'I was about to call you. You looked great. And the last shot of you all dancing in the rain made me laugh out loud.'

'Thanks,' I said. I felt as high as a kite. 'So you can tell Eleanor mission almost accomplished.'

'Mission accomplished? What mission?'

'Made you laugh. Cheered you up.' Oh God, *ohGod-ohGodohGodddd* I thought as I heard the words come out of my mouth and I realised it was too late to take them back.

'What do you mean?' William asked.

'Mean? Oh. Yeah. Nothing, really. Talking my usual rubbish. Just I'm glad I made you laugh. Er . . . we can celebrate at the weekend. If you . . . I mean, do you still . . .?' It was coming out all wrong and it wasn't helped by the ominous silence at the other end. 'William, are you still there?'

'Yes. I'm still here.'

'So do you still want to meet up at the weekend?'

'Doubt it. Eleanor's not good at the moment. You said something about her. Mission accomplished? What's she got to do with this?'

'Eleanor? Nothing. Not really. Me blabbing. Sorry. I don't know what I'm talking about. Stupid.'

'I'll ask her to tell me. And she will.'

I wanted the floor to open up and swallow me. Why had I opened my big stupid mouth? Stupid Stupid. 'No, please don't. Look, it's nothing. Not really. OK. Look. Just she said you'd been a bit down and that I should cheer you up. You know, she was looking after you like you look after her.'

More silence.

'So you . . . everything . . . it's all been because Eleanor asked you?' asked William finally.

'*Nooooo*. Course not. I *wanted* to. I've enjoyed . . . the . . . the contact we've had. Everything.'

'OK,' said William and the tone of his voice was cool. 'Let's get one thing clear and that is, I'm OK. I don't *need* cheering up. I am not a saddo who you need to feel sorry for just because my sister is ill. I can look after myself.'

'Oh, please don't tell Eleanor that I told you. She asked me not to tell you. I . . . I think she only wanted you to be OK.'

'I won't say anything,' he said. 'Bye then.'

And then he hung up.

I felt numb as I sat back on my bed. Hell, I thought. If only I could wipe out the last few minutes. Rewind the tape. Delete. I felt so frustrated. I wanted to kick myself or the wall or something.

'Arrghhhhhhhhhhhhhhhhhhhhhhhhhhhh,' I yelled and punched my pillows with all my might.

Mum came running down the corridor and rushed in.

'What's the matter? I heard you yell?' she asked as she looked around. 'Are you all right?'

'I am the most *stupid* idiot in the world and I should have my mouth taped up.'

'Why? What's happened?'

I turned over and faced the wall. 'Nothing,' I said.

Mum sighed. 'Nothing?'

I turned back to her, nodded and acted out zipping my lips. 'I've already said too much.'

'Oh, Nesta . . .'

I unzipped my lips. 'Sorry. Shouldn't have yelled. Moment of madness. Passed now. Need to be alone.'

Mum rolled her eyes. 'OK . . . but you know I'm here if you need me?'

I nodded again. Inwardly I vowed not to tell anyone about what I'd just said to William. It was so stupid and I didn't want to hear the inevitable reactions. Oh noooo. Nesta, you *didn't*? You *idiot*, etc. etc. I didn't want the looks that I knew they'd give me and each other – as if to say, oh well, that's what we've come to expect from Big Mouth Nesta. She's always putting her foot in it. Never stops to think before she speaks. She's so insensitive.

And it was true but this time, *this* time, I'd really blown it.

Tickets started to sell.

Donations started to come in.

By the following Wednesday, we had sold almost five hundred of the tickets and were having to have another batch printed. There was even talk that we might have to put a marquee in the car park next to the hall where the dance was being held to cope with the overflow of people.

After school on Wednesday, I met up with the girls at Banner's café in Crouch End to have a quick run-through the plans for Saturday night. We got a table at the back in one of the booths that feels as if you're a private compartment in an old-fashioned train.

'Music,' I said as I went through my list.

'Check,' said Izzie. 'Ben's got it sorted with the band. DJ Diggie will be there early to set up his system and Steve has done a fab soundtrack for the fashion show. His friend Mark will work the sound system while Steve takes photos out front and I think another friend is going to video it all.'

'Excellent job, Izzie. You've done brilliantly getting all that organised. Clothes?'

'Check,' said Lucy. 'We have some fabulous things for Star to choose from. And the local dry cleaners cleaned all the donations from the charity shops free of charge, so that's brillopad.'

'You guys have been so great. All of you,' I said as I could see how hard they'd all worked and I thought that they deserved to be told so. My mum is always saying, give credit where it's due so I try to do that. 'Other models?'

'*Other* models? Besides Star, you mean?' asked TJ.

'Er . . . yeah, no . . .'

'Yes, I have a list here,' said Lucy.

I felt awkward for a moment as I assumed that they'd automatically want me to be one of the models but Lucy hadn't mentioned it. My disappointment must have shown on my face as Izzie picked up on it immediately.

'Oh!' she said. 'Nesta. Did you want to model?'

'Not necessarily but – hey, yeah. Why not? I mean, I'm not being big-headed or anything but you know, people are always saying I could have been one and I did blag my way into Olympia pretending that I was one and no one asked any questions and . . .' It felt myself trailing off because it felt weird explaining myself to my best friends. I'd have thought that they would have taken it as read.

'It's not that,' said Izzie. 'Of course you'd be a fantastic model. And so would Lucy and TJ. But there's so much other stuff to do and we thought that – well, you've done so much. Organised so much. We didn't think you'd want to model as *well*.'

But that will be the best bit, I thought. I'd had visions of myself looking fab and coming down the catwalk with Star and everyone would be saying, Hey, that's Nesta Williams. She's the one behind all this you know and some of it might get back to William and when he heard how hard I'd worked, he wouldn't hate me as much as I was sure he did. But then . . . if I wasn't wanted . . .

'I have a list of about thirty people who want to model,' said Lucy. 'I thought it would be great to get as many as possible up there.'

'And we thought, let's not go for the obvious models,' said Izzie. 'Let's let everyone have a go. Short, plump, whatever. Show that you don't have to be tall and skinny to look good. With the right hair, make-up and clothes everyone can look great. And real girls are more "in" this year anyway, aren't they?'

'Yeah,' said Lucy. 'It would be a good message to have girls who looked like girls and not beanpoles who starve themselves.'

I'd been voted out and I wasn't sure how I felt about it. It was to have been my moment of glory and I already had an outfit that Lucy made for me last year picked out. I decided not to let on that I was peeved about it and then see if later, I could talk them into letting me do it.

'OK. Cool. Funds?' I asked trying to act as if I wasn't bothered at all.

'Check,' said TJ. 'We're doing well. We've sold five hundred tickets. At eight pounds each, that's four thousand and with other bits that will come in on the night, it will be closer to five thousand.'

'Is that all?' I groaned. 'After all my effort, we're still nowhere near the goal.'

Izzie looked surprised. '*Your* effort?'

'Er . . . *our* effort,' corrected Lucy.

'Yeah. Course, I mean . . . *our* effort,' I stuttered. 'That's what I meant. You know it was.' And then I thought I'd gone out of my way to thank everyone for their efforts but no one had acknowledged my contribution at all. 'Although it was *my* idea to get Star.'

'Yeah, but it was a joint effort in the end,' said Izzie.

'Yeah, but it was my mum who sent the camera crew,' I said.

'So what? Lucy's been up late every night this week sewing,' said Izzie. 'And TJ's been holding quiz nights and all sorts of sports activities to raise money. And half the school have been involved in one way or other. It doesn't all revolve around you.'

'I know that and I said I thought you'd all been totally brill but . . .'

'Hold on a mo,' said TJ. 'Look, it doesn't matter who did what. Come on, you guys, let's not fall out. It's not about us or anyone else taking the glory.'

We all agreed. I decided that we must all be tired with all the late nights but I could see Lucy and Izzie giving me strange looks and the atmosphere had soured. It wasn't fair. I wasn't trying to take all the credit, not exactly. I just didn't think that anyone had appreciated how hard I'd worked too.

When the others got up to go, I hung back.

'Are you coming?' asked Izzie.

'Nah. Got a few more notes to make,' I said. 'Last minute things, you know.'

'Suit yourself,' said Lucy and left with Izzie and TJ.

They hate me. I could tell. They were going to go out to the bus stop and talk about me and how I wanted to take all the credit and how I was self-obsessed. But I wasn't. Well, only a bit. I felt peeved. It had all been my idea and if it hadn't been for me, maybe there would still only have been ten tickets sold for the stupid dance. It wouldn't hurt anyone to acknowledge that an incy wincy bit.

As I sat there feeling sorry for myself, I saw TJ come back in. 'You all right, Nesta?' she asked, as she took a seat opposite.

'Yeah.'

'Mind if I stay for a while too,' she said as she pulled out a note pad. 'I got a few things to go over.'

'Whatever.'

'You're mad with us,' she said. 'I can tell. Why?'

'No, I'm not. I'm fine.'

'Liar. You've gone all serious and intense. Come on. Spill. You know the saying, friends listen to what you say but best friends listen to what you don't say. Well. I'm one of your best friends and there's something that you're not saying.'

'Nah, nothing. Just feel a bit weird. It's probably something hormonal.'

'Is your period due?

'No, but you know me, if I've not got PMT, I've got actual period pain or post-period pain or mid-period pain or pre-PMT or pre-pre-PMT.'

TJ smiled and began to sing, *'Sometime's it's hard to be a woman . . .'*

'Tell me about it,' I said. 'Nah. Just a bit tired, I guess.'

'And that's all?' asked TJ. 'Nothing else bothering you?'

'No. Yeah. Just . . . well . . . I'm not trying to take the credit or anything but sometimes I think that you guys misunderstand me. You don't get me. I'm only trying to do my best and it's not good enough.'

TJ listened patiently as I rambled on and on and finally admitted that I'd like to model in the show.

'Then you should have said, you eejit,' said TJ. 'We're not mind-readers. We thought you might enjoy the evening off to watch the show without having to worry about anything. We do appreciate what you've done and thought a night off would be what you wanted.'

'Oh.' That hadn't occurred to me. I'd thought they were keeping me out because they thought I was getting too big for my boots.

'And what about William Lewis?' she asked. 'Sure he's not bothering you? Is he coming to the dance?'

I'd kept to my vow and hadn't told the girls that I'd totally blown it with William. I still felt such a fool about blabbing Eleanor's secret request to him and didn't want to share it with anyone.

'Probably not,' I said. 'I think he'll be with his sister.'

'So what's happening?' asked TJ. 'Why haven't you met up?'

I shrugged. 'Um . . . his sister is his priority at the moment. I think that they're very close. Before he went to Spain, he told me that she often wants him with her when she's low because he doesn't get all emotional. He said that his parents, his mum in particular, finds it hard not to show her feelings when Eleanor is bad and seeing her mum upset freaks Eleanor out. I guess he manages to act more normal which is why Eleanor always asks him to be with her. He can go and stay over at the hospice so that at least she has company.'

'Yeah,' said TJ. 'A familiar face. I can understand that. Meeting them has made me really understand what the hospice is about. I mean, it must be scary going through what she's going through on her own. There must be times when she thinks, why me? And it must be very lonely as no one can have your treatment for you but at least, if people can stay over, there's someone there.'

'Yeah.'

'Like if one of us was ill,' said TJ. 'Or one of our family, I'd so want to have a friendly face in there with me and in most hospitals, it's an hour at visiting time and then you're on your own.'

I nodded. She'd reminded me what all our efforts were about. What had I been thinking, seeking credit for what we'd been doing? I felt mean and selfish. Sometimes I really hate myself. Like, why couldn't I be selfless and nice like Mother Theresa was? Everything I did was wrong or for the wrong reasons. Everything I said was wrong or came out the wrong way. Sudden tears pricked my eyes at the same time as Lucy and Izzie reappeared at the table.

'Hey, what is it?' asked Lucy as she slid next to TJ.

'I am mean and selfish,' I said.

'No, you're not,' she said. 'You're amazing. We all think that you're amazing. In fact, we were just saying that at the bus stop which is why we came back in. You are one of life's doers. You make things happen.'

'Yeah,' said Izzie as she slid in next to me and put her arm round me. 'And we should have told you. You're right. If it wasn't for you, most of what's been happening lately wouldn't have happened.'

'Yeah, you're like . . . a warrior queen,' said TJ. 'Boudicca, Queen of the Icini leading the troops.'

'Yeah. All hail, Queen Nesta of the Cappuccini . . .' Lucy started.

By now, tears were flooding down my cheeks. 'Oh noooo *dooooon't* . . . Sorry, sorry,' I sobbed as I scrabbled in my pocket for a tissue. 'Please don't . . .'

Izzie slid in next to me and began to sing. 'Oh, darling Nesta, we think you're so top, you get people going and now we can't stop . . .'

And then I began to laugh and then I didn't know if I was laughing or crying.

'What?' asked Lucy, looking around in bewilderment. 'Why's she crying? Why are you crying, Nesta? Don't cry. I hate seeing you cry. We were trying to tell you that we do appreciate your efforts, we really do.'

'Thanks but . . . I . . . just . . . before . . . I . . . oh never mind . . .' I blustered. I was crying because it felt like a dam had burst and I couldn't stop the tears coming and I was laughing because there they were, my mates giving me praise and credit and I suddenly realised that I didn't actually want it. I really, *really* didn't.

Friends listen to what you say.
Best friends listen to what you don't say.

Chapter 15

Sorry

'It's show time, folks,' said Tony as he poked his head around my door, then came into my room. He looked as if he'd stepped out of a limo at the Oscars in a black suit, white shirt and bow tie. 'Hey, Mum's gone to bring the car round to take us to the hall. Why aren't you ready?'

'I am,' I said and got up to squeeze past him into the hall.

'Excuse me,' he said as he looked at me in my jeans and T-shirt with disapproval, 'but where's the bling? The fab dress? Come on Nesta. This is your night. It's what you've been working for.'

'But it's *not* my night,' I said. 'Don't say that. I'll come and help set up and then I'm coming home.'

'Oh, for heaven's sake,' sighed Tony. 'One boy gives you the silent treatment and you become a recluse. Come on, Nesta, get over it.'

'Boy? What boy? No. It's not that. And he hasn't given me the silent treatment, not exactly. You don't understand . . .'

'No, I don't but I do know that he hasn't called here this week and you've been going round with a long face. Come on, Nesta. A chance to dress up and strut your stuff and you choose to wear your jeans? Are you hoping that a fairy godmother is going to turn up and wave a wand?'

'No. I'm just not in the mood, that's all.'

'Suit yourself,' said Tony. 'But I can tell you now that the girls aren't going to like it.'

'Don't care,' I said.

I didn't. I just wanted to get the night over with and then get back home. I'd been feeling lousy since my last fatal call with William and I'd tried to phone him since, but he wouldn't speak to me. I'd thought a lot about things since the last meeting in Banner's when the girls went out of their way to make me feel appreciated. I hadn't said anything to them at the time but their praise and kind comments had exactly the opposite effect.

I had realised that on top of being a big mouth that I was also a great big-headed show-off. Always wanting to be the centre of attention. Always wanting recognition. I hated myself. I'd got it all wrong. Wanting to help for all the wrong reasons. So that it would reflect well on me. And now I wanted to be quiet. I'd begun to wish I'd never got involved with charity work. I'd had nothing but trouble since I started it. In future, I would keep my head down, give anonymous donations and stay out of the limelight.

Mum dropped Tony and me at the hall and went off to get changed herself, collect Dad and come back later.

Everyone who was involved was there early and like Tony

were dressed to the nines ready for the activities to begin. The doors were due to open at seven, the fashion show was to start at eight and then it would be time for the band and the disco. It was a hive of activity with everyone dashing about and bumping into each other as they went about their various tasks: Ben and the band members setting up the sound system; Lucy in a room at the back putting the clothes for the show on rails in the order they were to be shown; Izzie organising a dressing area of sorts with make-up and hair brushes laid out. Lal and his mates setting out chairs around the main hall. Tony and his mate Stu had put fairy lights round the hall porch and laid out a red carpet from the car park to the entrance so that it would look like an awards' night in Hollywood. Steve was ready with his camera to take shots of people as they arrived. And TJ was set up to collect tickets at the front door. In every part of the hall, there was an air of anticipation and excitement. Except for me.

'Hey, Nesta,' said Lucy. 'You brought your outfit to change into?'

'Er, not exactly. Er . . . later. Hey. You look great.'

She did. They all did. It was bling city because everyone had taken the Diamond Destiny theme seriously and turned up dripping jewels in fab chokers and tiaras and earrings. Lucy was wearing a gorgeous silver grey sleeveless sheath dress that she'd found on a stall selling vintage clothes in Portobello Road. Very 1920s' elegant. It was made from the finest silk, cut on the bias and probably only Lucy would have been able to get into it as it was so tiny. It was as if it was made for her. Round her neck she had a wide diamanté choker and her hair was up at the back like a real movie star. Tony looked as if he was going to pass out when he saw her as she really did look Class A. Izzie was wearing one of her old favourites: a long black velvet dress and like Lucy, she also had a diamante choker round her neck. With her hair loose and over her shoulders and wearing a deep red lipstick, she looked like the ultimate glam Goth rock chick. And TJ had let Lucy dress her. She looked absolutely stunning in black trousers and a top that Lucy had made for her and diamante earrings. The top was a purple Basque with a zip down the front and no straps. She looked incredibly sophisticated and sexy. All the boys were ogling her chest as if their eyes were glued to it and after a while, she decided that it was too embarrassing and went and put her fleece on until the dancing started later.

Seeing them all looking so glamorous made me feel that I was missing out as usually I like nothing better than to dress up. But the feeling only lasted a minute. What was the point when the only boy that I was interested in wasn't even speaking to me?

Even Miss Watkins had made an effort and was wearing a long royal blue dress and a tiara. Sadly the shapeless dress resembled a tent and the tiara kept slipping over one of her eyes but at least she'd got into the spirit of things which was more than I had done.

At seven-thirty, she called me over from where I was helping Lucy run through the order of the clothes.

'Nesta, Star Axford's here,' she said. 'You're going to look after her aren't you?'

I looked over at Lucy. 'Oh, we didn't decide? Um . . . who should do it?'

'You go for it,' called Lucy. 'We're all busy.'

I raced out to the front to greet Star who was chatting to TJ at the ticket table and she gave me a big smile when she saw me.

'Hey you,' she said. 'We meet again.'

'Yes. And thank you so much for coming. It's totally brilliant of you.'

'So where do you want me?'

'We haven't got a proper dressing room so everyone's piled into a cloakroom area at the back but I can show you to the caretaker's room next door to that if you want some peace and quiet for a while.'

'Lead the way,' she said, then handed me a large Chanel carrier bag. 'And I brought some cast-offs with me as I'd like to donate something as well as my time. A few clothes for the show. In fact, we look about the same size so maybe you could model them.'

'Wow, thanks,' I said. 'I'll give them to my friend Lucy as she's in charge of that side of things but I . . . I'm not modelling tonight. I . . . I'm helping organise things and I'm not staying.'

'Oh, shame,' said Star as she followed me across the hall. 'I'd have thought you'd have been perfect.'

Once inside the small office, I showed her a few things we had put out ready for her. Water. A bowl of fruit. A box of tissues.

'Sorry we don't have much,' I said as I poured her some water. 'We weren't sure what you'd like. Um. Shall I organise someone to go and get you some champagne?'

She took the water and sat behind the desk. 'I don't drink if I'm doing a show so this is fine. Thanks.'

'So what's it like being a model?' I asked. 'I mean, really like?'

Star smiled. 'You'd be surprised. Some places don't offer you anything, not even a glass of water, not even a place to change. So it's mixed. There are good days and bad days, like most jobs. There's a lot of waiting around in strange places. It's not all bright lights and glamour. There's a lot of schlepping around, waiting at airports – all of that but in the main, I love it.'

'Your agent said that you do loads of these types of events . . .'

'Not exactly,' she said. 'Depends on my schedule. I do some.'

'Why?'

Star shrugged. 'I guess it's because . . . I don't know, it's hard to explain. I . . . I know I'm in a privileged position. I want to give something back. And this is one way. Simple as that. Why did you get involved?'

'Because I'm a show-off and I want everyone to think I'm great,' I said.

Star almost spat her water out as she burst out laughing.

'It's true. First I got involved to impress some boy but also because I'm a freaking great show off and want everyone to think I'm a fab kind person who cares about others. Nesta Williams. Miss Do Goody Two Shoes. But I'm a fake. I'm rubbish and my motives are purely selfish.'

Star laughed again. 'Well, at least you're honest.'

'Honest about being a mess.'

Star put her hand on my shoulder. 'Hey, don't be so hard on yourself, Nesta. You shouldn't worry about your intentions too much. You're doing *something* and that's better than nothing. I'm sure loads of people get involved for all sorts of reasons. Yeah, some to impress others. Others so that they don't feel guilty about what they've got. Sometimes I think that's part of the reason I do it. Because I feel guilty that I have so much. In the end though, I reckon it's all about balance. Enjoy your life but remember to give something back. That's all. Don't think about it too much. Keep it simple.'

'Yeah. Maybe.' Simple for her, I thought.

'So. Who's this boy you wanted to impress?' asked Star.

'His name is William and I really like him . . .'

Star was so easy to talk to that I found myself telling her the whole story right up to how he thought I was only bothering with him because his sister had asked me to.

'. . . and that's not exactly true,' I finished. 'I'd have wanted to see him even if she hadn't asked me.'

'So tell him that,' said Star.

I shook my head. 'Nah. He said he didn't need me feeling sorry for him. He couldn't have been clearer.'

'Do you have his number?'

I nodded.

'So call him,' said Star. 'Give him a chance. Give *yourself* a chance.'

'But I have and he won't pick up . . .'

'Allow for time, Nesta. He may have calmed down by now.'

I shook my head. 'Doubt it and anyway, it's all my fault and I'm probably getting what I deserve.'

Star shook her head. 'People say things they don't mean all

the time in the heat of the moment. People make mistakes. Don't let that stop you trying to make it right again.'

'It's too late,' I said. 'I heard his tone of voice . . . Brrrrr. It was c–c–cold.'

'Coward,' said Star. 'I've got a sister your age. Lia. She was really into this guy and thought that he had been messing about behind her back so she wouldn't speak to him. Actually he hadn't but she didn't know that at the time. Thing is, he didn't give up when she wouldn't take his calls. He kept trying and trying until she gave in.'

'And then what happened?'

'They got back together. Both realised they were being stupid and were miserable without each other. So *call* him.'

'But I *have* . . .'

'So call him again. I dare you. Remember the saying, fortune favours the brave. Don't let fear of rejection stop you. Anyway, what have you got to lose?'

That was true. What did I have to lose? Nothing.

As it got closer to the time for the show, I showed Star where Lucy and the models were getting ready then went out into the car park to call William.

I took a deep breath, punched in his number and waited. I could feel my heart thumping in my chest as I listened to the phone ring. Part of me didn't want him to be there as I was scared that he'd give me an earful. And part of me wanted him to pick up and tell me that it was all OK and had all been a huge misunderstanding and that he couldn't stop thinking about me and that I haunted his dreams. Or something like that.

A few moments later, he picked up.

'Ah . . . ah . . .' I stuttered. Oh God, I thought. I've done a TJ and gone blank. Wargh! This doesn't happen to me.

'Hello. *Hello?*' said William. 'Is there anybody there?'

'Ah . . . Yes. Um. Hi, William. This is Nesta.'

'Oh you . . .'

'Don't hang up! And before you say anything,' I began, and then talked as fast as I could. 'I want to say I'm sorry, actually no I'm not. I haven't got anything to be sorry for . . .'

'You've phoned to say that you're sorry but you're not?'

'Yeah. No. Um. See it's like this. I . . . yes, Eleanor did ask me to cheer you up but . . . actually even if she hadn't asked me to, I would have wanted to. Actually no. That's not right. Not cheer you up. That's not what I wanted to do at all.'

'Nesta. What are you on about? Sorry. Not sorry. Cheer me up. Not cheer me up. What?'

'Yeah. No. Not cheer you up. You said you don't need it and I agree. I mean I don't think that you look miserable, so why would you need cheering up? Actually no, that's probably wrong. You probably do some of the time as your situation must be very hard sometimes with your sister and you probably don't show it being a boy and they don't like to show their feelings sometimes . . . oh . . . what I'm trying to say is. . . oh Dunking Doughnuts! Can we start again? I . . . I like you. I would like to see you again and would have liked to see you even if Eleanor hadn't said anything.'

There was a silence at the other end.

'So?' I prompted.

'So,' William finally said. 'Me too.'

'Me too what?'

'Me too, I would have wanted to see you but I was well peeved with Eleanor for sticking her oar in. I don't need her to do that.'

'I know. I have an older brother who always thinks he knows what's best for me. It can be very annoying but I think Eleanor was only trying to help.'

'Well, it didn't, did it?'

'No. But maybe . . . maybe it's not too late.'

'Maybe. And actually, I guess I did fly off the handle a bit. I tend to do that sometimes, react and shoot my mouth off.'

'What sign are you?' I asked.

'Aries,' he said. 'Why?'

'You sound a bit like me. I'm Leo with Aries rising.'

'What does that mean? Rising?'

'Um, you'd have to ask Izzie as she's our resident astrologer. But anyone with Aries in their chart tends to leap before they look kind of thing. As you said, shoot-their-mouth-off types of people.'

'Sounds familiar,' said William.

'So. You know tonight's the Diamond Destiny Dance?'

'Yeah.'

'Will you come?'

'Sure,' said William.

'Sure? Oh. OK. Brilliant.'

I heard William laugh at the other end. 'I was coming anyway,' he said.

'You were?'

'Yeah. Olivia got me tickets ages ago. Just you be thankful you have only one brother. I have two sisters, both of whom think they know what's best for me. And I wanted to see you in person. Find out if there was anything else that Eleanor asked you to do.'

'Nope, nothing else. So you're coming. Excellent,' I said.

'Yep. See you later then.'

As I turned to go back in, I was struck by how magical the hall looked with fairy lights twinkling around the door. It was a lovely warm evening. Cars were drawing up and people getting out. Cameras were flashing. Music was beginning to pound from inside.

Suddenly I got the feeling that it was going to be a great night.

Fortune favours the brave.

Chapter 16

Diamond Destiny Dance

'Hey Nesta, get over here,' called Lucy when I got back into the hall. 'Where have you been?'

'In the car park. Why? What's the matter?'

'Nothing. Not a problem. Just Star gave us these gorgeous clothes to model and no one back here can fit into them. I think they'd be perfect on you, though. Come and try. And hurry. We're due to start in five minutes.'

Gorgeous clothes? Understatement, I thought as I tried on one of the dresses. A white Armani evening dress with tiny straps. It was so elegant and fitted like a glove. I felt a million dollars in it. Next was a gorgeous floaty chiffon dress by Stella McCartney. Then a sophisticated Calvin Klein black dress slashed at the shoulder.

'You'll be the belle of the ball,' said Star as she got changed next to me.

'I can't believe you're getting rid of these,' I said.

Star shrugged. 'I have loads at home and quite honestly, when am I going to wear them all? Shopping at Sainsbury's? I don't think so.'

'Places, girls,' called Lucy as the music started up and Izzie signalled that everyone was in their seats and the show about to begin.

It was such a blast. Like a series of fantasies come true. Following Star out onto the catwalk. The flash of cameras. Mum and Dad cheering like mad. Boys ogling me. Classmates watching and clapping when I appeared. Izzie and TJ grinning like idiots out front. Lucy grinning like an idiot from backstage. And at the very back of the hall, a really gorgeous boy with collar length hair watching with quiet admiration. William. When I looked over at him, he smiled his killer watt smile and gave me the thumbs up.

It was all over so fast. Up and down the catwalk. In and out of clothes. Back out. More flashes from cameras in the audience. (Mainly my dad who beamed with pride every time I stepped out.)

After the fashion show, while all the models got changed, Izzie and TJ got up and did this hysterical double act where they auctioned off the clothes and items from the charity shop. It sounded like a riot from backstage – we could hear them really getting into the part of barrow boys.

'All wight, everyone,' said Izzie in her best Cockney accent. 'So what am I bid for this 'ere novel. It's a first edition. Probably worf loadsa money.'

People started bidding from the audience and soon the sale was up and running with bidders trying to outbid each other for the fun of it.

'Come on, you tight lot,' called TJ. 'What am I bid for this stunning skirt?'

'How about if you're in it?' called a dark-haired boy from the back of the hall.

I went to stand with Lucy at the edge of the stage behind Izzie and TJ and looked round for William. 'Hey look, Lucy,' I said. 'Eyes left. Cute boy alert. Just your type, he looks a bit like Tony.'

'Oh yeah,' said Lucy. 'No. Not *quite* as gorgeous as Tony but not bad.'

I patted her on the head. 'Poor thing,' I said. 'My brother clearly has you under some strange spell and all we can hope is that one day, you'll awaken and see sense.'

'Hey, I think that boy who called out must be Star's brother, Ollie,' Lucy continued. 'See, he's with Zac Axford, over there to the left, talking to my dad.' She pointed at a man who was standing at the back of the hall talking to Mr Lovering. He looked like a rock and roller. He was in his early forties with straggly dark hair and dressed in jeans and a leather jacket. 'Dad didn't waste much time getting talking to him. Star told me that he was coming and when I told Dad, he almost passed out with excitement. He has every one of his albums.'

'Hhmm,' I said as I watched Ollie banter with TJ over the skirt. 'Methinks that yonder Ollie fancies our TJ.'

Lucy glanced back at Ollie and nodded. 'Methinks you is

right,' she said. 'Good. TJ could do with a bit of buff boy attention.'

After the auction, it was time for the music and King Noz soon got the place rocking. I looked around for William in the hope that he'd ask me to dance but couldn't see him anywhere. Izzie did a number with the band and when she'd finished, Lucy's dad got up to join them as well. As he got to the stage, I saw that Zac Axford had followed him over and was saying something. Mr Lovering then beckoned Ben who went over to join them and nodded in recognition at Zac. Ben suddenly beamed, got up and handed Zac a guitar. Next thing we knew, Lucy's dad was up there with Zac Axford and both of them were playing with the band. It was incredible. The crowd went mad, dancing and stomping like there was no tomorrow. I didn't think it could get any better until I felt two hands slip round my waist from behind.

I turned to see that it was William. I was about to say something but he just pulled me back so that I was leaning against him, his hands still round my waist. The sensation of being so close to him made me feel as if I'd turned to liquid. I didn't want the moment to end. It felt so perfect, watching the band like a regular couple. It was only when they began to play a ballad and the pace slowed down that he pulled me to the edge of the crowd.

'I just want to say sorry for my big mouth again . . .' I started.

He leaned over, put a finger against my lips then pulled me to him and gave me a long-deep-to-the-tip-of-my-toes-and-back-again snog. Heavenly, heavenly, heaven.

★ ★ ★

At the end of the night, when everyone had gone, TJ, Lucy, Izzie and the Dopey Doreens piled into the caretaker's office. Miss Watkins made us tea and we sat around like a bunch of old businessmen to count the takings. I felt brilliant. William had left with Olivia but not before promising to call me in the morning. The future was looking bright.

'Four thousand five hundred,' said TJ who was doing the accounts. 'Cheque for fifty, excellent. Five pounds, ten pounds. Hey, it's looking good . . .'

And so she went on, five thousand. Six. The takings were good, but it didn't look as if we would make our target. Nowhere near. I couldn't help feeling disappointed and wished that there was more that I could have done.

Suddenly TJ's face registered shock. 'Ohmigod, ohmi*god*,' she said as she held up one cheque.

'What? What is it?' asked Miss Watkins.

TJ was speechless as she handed over the cheque. Miss Watkins glanced down at it and she too looked surprised.

Her face lit up. 'Ohmigod,' she said.

'*Whaaaaat?*' I asked.

Miss Watkins beamed. 'Our celebrity guest left us a little donation,' she said and she turned the cheque around so that we could all see. It was signed by Zac Axford and it was for the sum of forty-five *thousand* pounds.

Later, when everything was locked up, I went to sit with TJ, Izzie and Lucy on the wall in the car park while we waited for Lucy's dad to come back and taxi us all home.

'That was totally top,' said TJ as she moved over to make room for me between her and Lucy. 'And did you see the faces of the Dopey Doreens when Miss Watkins held that cheque up?'

'Yeah,' said Izzie. 'We showed them but they were cool in the end, weren't they? At least they had grace to say well done to everyone.'

'But you don't seem so thrilled, Nesta,' said Lucy. 'We *did* it. So what's the matter?'

I looked back at the hall. Only hours before, it had been so full of life, lights on, music blasting out of it. And now it was dark, silent, empty. I looked up at the sky. It was a clear night and up there in the heavens, the stars were twinkling down on us. I felt so small and insignificant.

'I *am* thrilled,' I said. 'Really. It's a great result. Just . . . now it's all over I can't help but think so what? So we raised the money. Big deal. A drop in the ocean. There's still so much pain the world.'

'Hey, Nesta's gone all deep on us,' teased Izzie. 'Usually it's you telling us to lighten up.'

'Yeah. Don't be sad, Nesta,' said Lucy. 'Not tonight. It's been a great night. It couldn't have gone better and you and William . . .'

'But that's just it. William. I really like him. And we're going to see each other. We have a future but I can't help thinking what about Eleanor? What kind of future has she got? What has she got to look forward to?'

The others fell quiet and I could see that I'd put a real dampener on their good mood.

'Sorry, guys,' I said. 'Can't help it. I feel sad. And small and helpless.'

Lucy put her arm through mine. 'I think we have to remember what Mrs Owen said. That day at the jumble sale, remember? Be happy. Do what you can, while you can. Be happy. Enjoy life. All aspects.'

'Yeah,' said Izzie as she linked arms with Lucy. 'Who knows how long we've all got? Any of us. It would be great if our birth certificate came like Mum's credit cards. You know, showing the date of issue *and* the date of expiry. Then we'd know. But we don't. Thing is to make the most of it while we're here and we're healthy.'

'Yeah,' said TJ as she linked my other arm. 'And while we've got each other.'

I felt my eyes fill up with tears. I was so lucky to have such great friends. It must be so hard for William knowing that he was going to lose his sister. I couldn't bear the thought of losing Izzie or TJ or Lucy or any of my family. But for the time being, here we were. My mates. On a wall in a car park in East Finchley under the stars. Who knows what life had in store for any of us. But one thing I did know and that was that summer was around the corner. I was going to do my best to appreciate every single second of it.

**The MATES, DATES series
by Cathy Hopkins:**

1. Mates, Dates and Inflatable Bras
2. Mates, Dates and Cosmic Kisses
3. Mates, Dates and Portobello Princesses
4. Mates, Dates and Sleepover Secrets
5. Mates, Dates and Sole Survivors
6. Mates, Dates and Mad Mistakes
7. Mates, Dates and Pulling Power
8. Mates, Dates and Tempting Trouble
9. Mates, Dates and Great Escapes
10. Mates, Dates and Chocolate Cheats
11. Mates, Dates and Diamond Destiny

Also available:
Mates, Dates Guide to Life

**The TRUTH, DARE, KISS OR PROMISE series
by Cathy Hopkins:**

1. White Lies and Barefaced Truths
2. Pop Princess
3. Teen Queens and Has-Beens
4. Starstruck
5. Double Dare
6. Midsummer Meltdown

Find out more at www.piccadillypress.co.uk

www.piccadillypress.co.uk

☆ The latest news on forthcoming books

☆ Chapter previews

☆ Author biographies

☆ Fun quizzes

☆ Reader reviews

☆ Competitions and fab prizes

☆ Book features and cool downloads

☆ And much, much more . . .

Log on and check it out!

Piccadilly Press